CREATIVE MATCHMAKER

CREATIVE MATCHMAKER

THE INSCRUTABLE PARIS BEAUFONT™ BOOK 6

SARAH NOFFKE

MICHAEL ANDERLE

LMBPN Publishing
PMB 196, 2540 South Maryland Pkwy
Las Vegas, NV 89109

Version 1.01, August 2021
eBook ISBN: 978-1-64971-951-5
Print ISBN: 978-1-64971-952-2

CHAPTER ONE

Nothing was worse than being reduced to Agent Ruby's current depths.

He was still going to use that title. Agent Ruby would call himself that even though he had to flee the Fairy Godmother Agency after Paris Beaufont and her worthless mortal uncle, who had been posing as a fairy, blew his cover. He'd returned the "favor" and blown Detective Nicholson's cover too, and that gave Agent Ruby a small amount of callous joy.

Agent Ruby hadn't stayed around FGA once he knew they could link him to Agent Topaz's death—but he did leave behind evidence that proved John Nicholson was a Mortal Seven and not the fairy he'd been masquerading as for fifteen years. It only took Agent Ruby a little digging, once he knew where to look to find out that John Nicholson was John Caraway, the owner of a rundown electronic repair shop in West Hollywood.

The pretend detective would have had to leave his job on Roya Lane too, the same as Agent Ruby. Unlike him though, John Caraway wasn't a fugitive, being hunted by the other agents at FGA and the authorities at the Fairy Law Enforcement Agency.

As soon as he realized that he'd lost the heart-shaped red ruby at the end of his silver ballpoint pen in the FLEA jail, Agent Ruby knew that all was lost. Losing that part of his magical instrument was more than enough to connect him to the location, Agent Topaz's murder, and much, much more. It was ironic to Agent Ruby that he'd gone to such lengths to cover his tracks on Agent Opal's death and FriendNet, only to leave behind the one thing that would undoubtedly tie him to everything.

Equally frustrating was that the plan to make cell phones addictive, thereby ruining relationships, had failed thanks to an intervention by some irritating dragonriders. The scientists who Agent Ruby had employed said that they'd jammed the signal and that undoing it would take time. Admitting defeat, Agent Ruby told the scientists not to bother.

He'd set his sights on something bigger. Something that wouldn't only destroy love. That had been the plan before, to take Saint Valentine down and seize his position. It hadn't worked. It had ruined Agent Ruby, taking away the one thing he wanted more than anything —to be Saint Valentine, ruling over all the fairy godmothers and agents.

Now the man once known as John Paul Williams had nothing to lose. Agent Ruby was going to destroy everything he couldn't have. Before, he simply wanted to bring the love meter to zero so the board would throw the current Saint Valentine out of office. Now Agent Ruby was going to take down the entire magical organization. If he couldn't have the position he'd longed for and the power he deserved, no one would have it.

There would be no love.

Agent Ruby wasn't only planning to take down Saint Valentine and Matters of the Heart. He had set his sights on ending the Fairy Godmother Agency and every agent within it. Even that wasn't enough. No, Agent Ruby wouldn't stop until the fairy godmothers were no more, and that started with Happily Ever After College. Most importantly, Agent Ruby was taking down Paris Beaufont.

He wouldn't rest until he ruined that halfling with demon blood. Killing her wasn't enough. He'd had everything he ever wanted stolen from him thanks to her meddling. Only once she'd lost all that *she* loved would he be happy. Better still, it was the girl with demon blood who'd given Agent Ruby the idea for her and the fairy godmothers' destruction.

Still wearing the black suit that was the uniform of the fairy godmother agents, Ruby nearly tripped as he stepped across a cesspool filled with disgusting liquid. He covered his nose and mouth with the handkerchief with the old initials: JPW. The putrid smell of rot and sewer would only get worse, Agent Ruby knew.

The whole of Minneapolis smelled disgusting for many reasons. Most thought it was the dirty lakes or the pollution, but they were wrong. It was because the demon population was out of control in the northern city. In the last fifteen years, demons had mostly gone unchecked. They thrived in the cold weather and preferred feasting off quaint country bumpkins who lived on the outskirts of the metropolitan area.

Agent Ruby knew all this because of his time working at FGA. Keeping demons away from fairy godmothers was crucial to their success. As an expert agent, Ruby had protected his fairy godmothers. Now he'd do the exact opposite and feed them to the soul-sucking demons. That's what they deserved…Paris Beaufont wouldn't get off so easily, though. He had something much more sinister planned for her.

With a flick of his silver ballpoint pen, the graffiti-covered door flew off the hinges. The condemned house smelled of rot, more so than the streets around it. The three demons Agent Ruby had tracked there all jumped to their feet, baring teeth that contrasted greatly against their red skin.

Demons went unnoticed by mortals because they didn't see what they didn't want to be real. That made it easier for the soul-suckers to sweep in and do what they did best—steal joy and love from people. Magicians saw demons, but they also could end them, so the latter stayed away from the former unless wanting to turn them into one of their own. Plus, magicians were less affected by the assault on emotions that demons did to their prey. Fairies couldn't become demons because they were too pure in that regard—made to be creative.

However, demons loved nothing more than feasting on fairies because they usually had so many positive emotions. That's why protecting the fairy godmothers had been such a job. At Happily Ever After College, a demon couldn't enter the grounds since it existed in a bubble. Similarly, FGA and Matters of the Heart were in a protected skyscraper in New York City. Only agents and fairy godmothers and those with special invitations could get onto the premises.

Agent Ruby might be an outlaw, with many from Matters of the Heart searching for him. However, he still had access to FGA and Happily Ever After College. It was risky entering those locations, but Agent Ruby had nothing left to lose. This was his plan to take everything down with him, so he didn't care if they caught him in the end. It would be too late by then anyway. He also had a way to stay hidden on the grounds of Happily Ever After College, taking a front-row seat as he destroyed all the fairy godmothers and Paris Beaufont.

A growl ripped from the closest demon's mouth, drool running down his pointy chin with a horn on its end. The monster was bald and also had horns on the side of its round head. His companions flanking him were equally hideous with their black fingernails, horns, and red eyes. Demons could have passed for goths with implants and strange piercing addictions at a rave and probably did when a mortal noticed them.

The other two hissed as the one in front started for Agent Ruby. He held up a single hand in a commanding fashion and dared to smile at the monster.

"I have a proposition for you," he began in a low voice, full of confidence. "Don't leech me. Don't harm me. I will deliver you a feast unlike any other you've ever had."

CHAPTER TWO

"I can't believe he lost his job." Paris looked in her vanity's mirror and tossed her hair to the side.

Faraday nodded over her shoulder, sitting on the dresser behind her. "I know. But he sounded hopeful, right?"

"Yeah." Paris turned away from her appearance and looked around her room in the mansion of Happily Ever After College, but not to search for anything. It was so different from the place she'd shared with her Uncle John for all her life and yet the same. Small. Modest. Lacking personal effects.

"He's been wanting to return to the mortal world, don't you think?" Faraday scratched his ear with his back leg.

"Yeah, I think so," Paris answered. "I mean, he gave up his life to raise me when my parents disappeared in the vortex. Uncle John abandoned his electronic repair shop, his girlfriend, his life. Maybe it's a blessing that the fairies learned he's not one of them, and he has to leave his job as a detective for FLEA. Still, that's also been his life for the last fifteen years, and it must be difficult for him to up and leave it. He can't even be on Roya Lane anymore since mortals aren't supposed to be there."

"I think we have to count our victories here," Faraday offered.

"John did all of this so he could keep you safe and he has. The long goal was to bring your parents back, which you did—"

"We did," Paris corrected.

The talking squirrel grinned proudly. "We did. Your uncle, as much as he enjoyed his job as a detective, had a very stressful, demanding time with it. Now he has a reason to return to his work repairing electronics, which he loved. It didn't happen on his terms, but it's happened at an acceptable time because your parents are ready to take back their positions as Warriors for the House of Fourteen, so it's fine if all the truths come out. Everything will soon return to the way it used to be."

Paris sighed, trying to muster a nod. "Yeah, it's just that it's returning to how things were before I was born or before I can remember. I don't know what Uncle John's normal was. I don't know what my parents' lives were like before everything got turned upside-down.

"Even Aunt Sophia and Uncle Clark have different lives from before the Deadly Shadow came along and changed everything. I think things will return to how they used to be, as much as they can, but the only thing different will be me. I'm the one who doesn't know who the people in my life used to be."

Faraday offered her a thoughtful look, strange wisdom in his eyes. "I think we never know who people were before we entered their lives. If we're anyone at all, we change their lives so they *are* never the same. It's not a bad thing that you had such an impact on everyone's life. You're the first halfling magician and fairy in history. You're special. If you didn't change everything by entering this world, I'd be concerned."

Paris smiled at her friend, grateful for his words. "Speaking of changing lives, you have to feel pretty awesome after saving love from cell phone addiction. That was some impressive nerdy stuff you did to stop that signal from the satellite. Everyone at the college knows about it. A lot of the girls have been asking if I can get your autograph."

Faraday snickered, waving his paw dismissively. "That's silly. I'm a nobody."

"You saved love making the meter recover," Paris countered. "You're kind of a big deal. Headmistress Starr says she's working with Wilfred to get you a lab. I hear it's going to be on the mansion's third floor."

The squirrel's eyes widened. "The third floor. But that's restricted to faculty and staff."

Paris laughed. "When has 'restricted' ever stopped you? I'm pretty sure if there's yellow tape around something, you think of it as an invitation to enter."

He nodded with a giggle. "It's true. I've been too busy with other things to investigate the third floor, though. I think it was only restricted for privacy purposes, not for a cool conspiracy reason."

Paris rolled her eyes. "Yeah, if there's not a ghost haunting it or malfunctioning magitech butlers, you're not interested."

"It's true," Faraday chirped, rocking forward on his hind legs and back again. "Once I have my lab, I can do all sorts of things."

"Like make me peanut brittle?" Paris joked, glancing at her image in the mirror again. There was little hope for her hair, which wanted to be schizophrenic, going straight in some places and curly in others.

"I'm allergic to peanuts, so no," Faraday answered. "I was thinking of science experiments. I was debating replicating the double-slit experiment. Oh! And there's one on random number generators. I'll need a few participants for that. Do you think some of the students would be willing to volunteer?"

"I think if you ask them to bake you cookies, you'll have a few hundred batches at our door," Paris teased.

Faraday blushed. "Well, I don't want cookies. I'm not a big sweets fan. I could use some test subjects, though."

"I wouldn't sell it like that," Paris offered. "Tell them that you have a grand opportunity for them that could help them make history for science. It's all about how you phrase things."

"Right," he replied. "Good thinking. Yes, the lab will enable me to help you with more things."

Paris sighed. "What kinds of things?"

"You know, fighting bad guys. Saving the world. Recovering love. Whatever you need, Paris. I'm here to help."

She straightened her leather jacket. "Well, I'm not sure about all that. I have my parents back. The love meter is recovering, and Agent Ruby is on the run. Hopefully, he doesn't cause any more problems for FGA."

"I wouldn't be too sure about that," Faraday cautioned.

"Why is that?"

"Well, he's going to be out for revenge now," Faraday explained. "You ruined him. You proved he was at the FLEA jail. Then you recommended they test the heart-shaped ruby he left behind. It connected him to all the spells he tried to plant on Agent Topaz, most importantly that he stole his pocket watch and used it to create the potion that murdered Agent Opal.

"Not to mention that Agent Ruby killed a man to cover his tracks. That's the sign of a desperate man. Do you think he'll go away now that Saint Valentine knows who he is?"

Paris paused, tension constricting her throat for a moment. "Good point. So you don't think we've seen the last of Agent Ruby then?"

"Not by a long shot." Faraday hopped off the dresser to the windowsill. "Which is why I'll get to work on things to help."

"You don't know what to help with yet." Paris made for the door, the smell of bacon and freshly brewed coffee downstairs leading the way.

"Oh, that's all right," Faraday stated with confidence. "I'll let my creativity lead the way. Often when I do, I find solutions before I know which problem they're for."

Paris regarded the squirrel, noticing the renewed sense of confidence he wore well. "Well, I like the idea of finding answers before problems. Maybe you can offer some before one of my exams tomorrow. I've never been good at tests."

"I draw the line at cheating," Faraday said sternly. "I'll help you save the world. I'll help you recover your parents from another dimension. I won't aid you in getting a score you don't deserve on an exam."

Paris rolled her eyes and put her hand on the doorknob. "Oh, that's where your moral code lies. Good to know. If something is off-limits, you're there. I don't have any socks without holes, and you don't lose sleep on that one. But your moral compass points in the right direction when it comes to helping me pass Magical Cooking."

"Cheating at passing," he corrected. "Yes. There's nothing more important than learning academics on your own. I'm doing you no favors by assisting you with bypassing the requirements."

"Well, then, I better get down to breakfast to grill Chef Ash on what will be on the exam since you'll be of zero help." She glanced skeptically at the squirrel.

"Grill…Chef Ash! Ha!"

Paris chuckled. "What are you going to do today?"

"Explore. I hear that the Bewilder Forest is quite a strange sight as it's regrowing. There are new species of plants and animals."

Paris tensed. "Yeah, my strange hybrid blood made for some unique stuff."

"You say that as if it's a problem."

"Well, you try having an entire forest regrowing thanks to your blood and changing the landscape of an entire college."

He sighed, looking out the window at the Enchanted Grounds of Happily Ever After College. "As if I could be so lucky."

"You're so weird," she joked.

"You too," he retorted.

"Well, try not to get into trouble with your exploring." Paris opened the door.

He nodded. "You too, Pare. Although I realize I'm asking a lot."

She grinned over her shoulder. "You're definitely asking too much. See you later."

"Later." Faraday hopped out the open window and scurried toward the brand-new forest, grown from the blood of a magician and a fairy with a tiny bit of demon.

CHAPTER THREE

Chef Ash was giving Hemingway a skeptical glare when Paris sat with her full plate of scrambled eggs, bacon, and an English muffin.

"I think hash browns are better with ketchup, not mustard." Chef Ash tucked his trademark pencil behind his ear.

"I think that I get to eat my hash browns the way I like." Hemingway squirted a fine line of yellow mustard over his food.

"You're doing that to get under my skin." Chef Ash leaned back in his chair and crossed his arms.

"Despite your propensity toward self-absorption," Hemingway began, picking up his fork. "I rarely do anything to get a rise out of you. I have better things to do with my time."

"Everything okay?" Paris raised an eyebrow at the two, not having seen them bickering like that before.

Chef Ash sighed dramatically. "Hemingway is ruining his food with mustard."

"I'm trying something new," Hemingway countered, taking a bite of his hash brown doused in yellow mustard before puckering his lips with disapproval. "Yeah, that's not so good."

"I told you." Chef Ash threw his head back.

"I'll tell you what ruins things," Christine remarked, entering the conversation in a conspiratorial whisper. She leaned forward as if she was about to relay a great secret. "People everywhere seem to think it's okay to wear mustard yellow. I see it everywhere. They think it's a warm, autumn color. First off, it's not autumn. Second, even if it were, no one looks good in mustard yellow. How can we make this stop?"

She turned to Paris. "You know important people. Can you get Mother Nature to put a swift halt to this? My eyes can't take it."

Paris laughed. "I think Mama Jamba has better things to do. I'm sorry, I think you'll have to ignore such fashion faux pas'."

"Easy for you to say," Christine replied. "You don't even care when you see people wearing overalls as if it isn't the biggest fashion crime ever to happen. What next? Are we all going to go around wearing baggy jumpsuits as though we borrowed clothes from a toddler? Is that really where we're heading!"

Paris' eyes widened. "You're really charged on this subject. Might I suggest you lay off the coffee?"

"Your suggestion has been noted." Christine grabbed her mug of black coffee as though Paris might steal it and swallowed a big gulp.

"Right, so no crazy going on here then," Paris said in a sing-song voice. "Did I not get the extra kick in my Wheaties this morning? What's going on with everyone?"

Hemingway's eyes connected with hers and he nodded, leaning forward. "The *others*, if you know what I mean, seem a little on edge this morning."

By "others," she believed he was referring to the fairies. They did seem to be more emotional than usual. More easily put off, whereas people like Chef Ash were usually cool even under pressure.

"Speaking of food." Paris tried to change the subject. "I hoped that you, Chef Ash, could give me a heads-up on the exam tomorrow. Like, what should I focus on studying?"

His fork clattered to the table when he deliberately dropped it. "I wish I could. I don't know what's on the exam."

"How?" Penny asked. Paris realized that she'd been there all along, hanging back as usual. "It's your class."

"It's complicated." Chef Ash retrieved his fork and speared it into his eggs as if they did something rude to him.

"Complicated how?" Hemingway asked.

"Complicated as in I don't want to talk about it," Chef Ash replied. "You'll find out soon enough."

Paris pushed her plate away, suddenly not hungry, having to deal with all the competing emotions. "Is something wrong?"

"Everything," Chef Ash replied, not at all his usual chipper self.

"Can I help?" Paris asked.

He shook his head. "You have enough on your plate."

"I don't," Paris stated. "I mean, Agent Ruby is gone. Faraday is back. Phones are fixed. My parents are about to reenter the world, and I get to be open about them with everyone else."

"Yeah, you're, like, the coolest," Christine gushed. "Start at the beginning and tell me every detail of what happened at the FLEA jail again. I can't believe you apprehended that rascal."

Paris shook her head. "I didn't. He got away after he assaulted my uncle."

"Who isn't a fairy," Penny asked for confirmation.

Paris nodded. "Yeah, and he had to step down as a detective for FLEA. Since I didn't apprehend Agent Ruby, he's out there doing who knows what. The deceitful fairy."

"I'm sure he's trying to get as far from Happily Ever After College and FGA as possible," Chef Ash offered. "I mean, he's a wanted fugitive. Saint Valentine will have every agent searching for him now."

"I'm not so sure," Paris said under her breath.

Catching her response, Hemingway perked up. "Why do you say that?"

"Well, it's something Faraday said," Paris answered.

"Oh, he's my hero," Christine exclaimed, clasping her hands to her chest as if they were talking about a rock star. "You can get him to sign my bra, right?"

"I don't think so," Paris replied before glancing at Hemingway. "He said something that makes me think a dangerous man such as Agent Ruby, who has nothing to lose, might be in the position to do something even more drastic than before."

"Even more drastic than killing a man?" Penny's fear was evident in her voice.

Paris nodded. "Exactly. It makes sense. He was willing to do so much to get power. Since that failed and he had to flee, well, who knows what he'll do now."

"Or maybe he'll want his freedom," Chef Ash stated. "You blew his cover, and he was going to do all that before to keep things hidden. Now he has nothing to gain."

"Yeah, but isn't a person like that the most dangerous?" Hemingway countered.

Paris nodded, Hemingway's words mirroring her thoughts. "Yeah, I think we're better off not discounting Agent Ruby yet. We should keep our eyes open."

"Oh, you're such a magician," Christine remarked. "Your type is always so paranoid."

"Magicians are rational," Hemingway countered. "They're simply more skeptical and guarded. It's not such a bad thing."

Paris offered him a grateful smile over her muffin as she took a bite. Knowing that secretly he was a magician made her appreciate the line he had to ride, like Uncle John. He understood the different parts of her that didn't operate like fairies. They were all emotions and feelings, whereas magicians were more practical in their approach. More calculated.

"Well, whatever." Christine pushed up from the table. "I wish I was a magician today because there's something wrong in the cosmos affecting fairies. I feel like Mercury is in retrograde, my mood ring is black, and I'm as emotional as a teenager. I'd cut someone to have your rational, even-keeled blood at this point."

Paris glanced around the dining room, noticing how many of the students seemed overly emotional. Many were ranting, crying, or seemed distraught in different ways. She had no idea what was going on at the college, but there was a problem brewing with the fairies. A problem that wasn't affecting her as a halfling or Hemingway as a magician. A problem that Paris needed to investigate.

CHAPTER FOUR

If Paris didn't already suspect that things at Happily Ever After College were off, she would have immediately jumped to that conclusion when she entered her Art of Love class. The vibe felt more like she was entering a funeral parlor than a session where they learned about love through literature, film, and art.

"Did everyone forget to take their antidepressants?" Paris asked Christine when she took her seat at the front of the class.

Her friend wiped a tear from her wet eyes and pointed at the movie projection playing on silent at the front of the room. "Did you watch our assignment?"

Paris glanced at the image of a man and a woman, her arms outstretched, and their faces held up to the wind as they stood at the bow of a ship cutting through choppy waters. "*Titanic*? Yeah, I watched it. Is that why everyone is crying?"

"He died!" Christine exclaimed, offense written on her face as if it was Paris' fault that Jack, Leonardo DiCaprio's character died.

Headmistress Willow Starr strode into the classroom, her eyes full of curiosity about the exclamation and all the tearful students. "What's going on?" She looked around.

"Oh, everyone lost their meds and are overreacting," Paris replied casually, looking from the fairy godmother to the projection.

"Some of us have hearts that break when romance fails!" Becky Montgomery said through a throat full of sobs.

"This is about the film you all were assigned to watch?" Willow asked, obviously as confused as Paris and thankfully not as emotional as the other fairies in the classroom. "You're all upset about *Titanic?*"

"They didn't end up together!" Becky wailed, sounding like she was getting worked up.

Paris had seen the film. It was good. Touching. Heartwarming. Yes, a little sad, but that wasn't the point, she felt. Now she thought the fairies had all missed the real message in the film. She turned halfway in her seat to look at the crying students behind her and the headmistress now at the front of the classroom.

"Sometimes romance isn't about happily ever afters," Paris began, earning a gasp from many. She continued over the whispers of protest. "Sometimes, it's about the journey and not about two people ending up together."

"How can you say that when you attend a college called Happily Ever After?" Becky challenged.

Paris sighed. "That's a name. A sentiment. Yes, we want our Cinderellas and Prince Charmings to end up together and have a lifetime of love. That's a goal. We also need to want to create love for the sake of people having it, even if for only a little while. It's like the old phrase that it's better to have loved and lost than never to have loved at all."

"That's atrocious!" Becky complained. "Another reason that a magician is unfit to be a fairy godmother."

"Actually, Paris is exactly right," Willow stated, cutting into the argument diplomatically as she strode forward, her blue gown swaying back and forth. "Maybe under past administrations, we only taught examples where love lasted through the decades. However, our current Saint Valentine has been flirting with new curricula and likes the idea of us studying romances of all types. There's much we can learn if we don't confine ourselves to the traditional stories of love."

She gave Becky a pointed look, a rare bit of defiance in the usually peaceful fairy godmother's eyes. "Paris will make an excellent fairy godmother because she's a halfling and has a unique perspective." She turned her attention to her. "Please, Paris, share your thoughts on the movie. I'd like to hear them."

"Well," Paris began, drawing out the word. "Even though Jack dies, his story is about sacrifice and passion. We learn that real love is worth the risk. We learn that we should never settle if our heart isn't in it. We also learn that there are no guarantees in this life. So you have to love with your entire heart and be grateful if true love bestows itself upon you, even for a short time.

"Wouldn't we all rather be blessed with the type of love that gives you butterflies and makes you feel high for a fleeting moment than given an unfulfilling relationship for a lifetime? I, for one, think a romance like in the movie inspires more love than an arranged marriage full of the customs of two stuffy aristocrats."

"Again, you're vying for us to match commoners," Becky scoffed.

Paris turned, leveling her gaze at her. "Yes, I think our efforts should focus on creating love for all people regardless of their financial status or lineage. I dare say that I think we should match people based on what feeds their soul. Maybe that means finding their Prince Charming or their Cinderella or a friend or a passion that's unrelated to a person at all. Love shouldn't only be about romance. Love is about so much more, and we've confined ourselves for too long."

Becky laughed rudely at Paris. "What you're talking about will never happen. FGA would never waste our time with such ridiculous missions."

"Not presently," Headmistress Willow stated. "However, I think that a more progressive movement is upon us. What Paris has mentioned isn't a bad idea. It's radical though, and FGA doesn't move fast when it comes to such things."

"For good reason," Becky replied. "The board would never approve it."

"We shall see," Willow said in a sing-song voice, a hint of something in her voice. "Tomorrow's exam will be in essay form. I expect to see a thorough understanding of the complexity of love as presented through various art forms." She paused, lowered her chin, and sighed. "Yes, Rebecca?"

Paris turned her head, noticing that Becky the Bully was waving.

"Mother says the board is requiring you to abide by strict student learning outcome guidelines for the exams," Becky said in a haughty voice.

"They have made their recommendations but can't overrule Saint Valentine," Willow replied in a clipped tone, her usual unending patience finally waning.

"I'm sure it's only a matter of time before that's not true," Becky stated in a snide tone.

"Saint Valentine, who has had to deal with many conflicts within FGA due to this Agent Ruby mess, is not concerned with the board or their recommendations, Rebecca. I'm not sure where you get your information, but I will remind you that your job is as a student here and not a faculty member, a board member for FGA, or anyone else of authority over the college. If I were you, I'd concern myself with your exams tomorrow, which will follow my standards and not those of the board."

Paris hid the victorious smile trying to show on her lips. She wanted to high-five Headmistress Starr or cheer for her retort but figured it was better to remain quiet. She'd never seen Willow like this. Something was heightening the emotions of the fairies at the college. She also suspected that the headmistress had run out of patience in regard to the Montgomery family and the prodding of the nosy FGA board.

CHAPTER FIVE

Paris groaned when she entered the ballroom for dancing lessons. It wasn't because she hadn't mastered the four types of dances she needed to demonstrate to pass her exam the next day. It wasn't even because Becky was glaring at her from across the ballroom. It was because the tailor, Juergen, was in attendance and doing another round of measurements and fittings for the ball gowns.

Paris didn't know how to get out of this whole thing. For the final graduation ceremony at Happily Ever After College, she had to wear the dress made for her, ballroom dance, and present many of the skills she was supposed to master before receiving her diploma. She was positive she'd throw up straight afterward, all over the sparkly blue ball gown.

"Miss Beaufont," Wilfred, the magitech AI butler said in a calm voice, waving Paris over with his white-gloved hand. "Juergen is busy fitting other ladies today so you can join me for today's lesson. You'll have to see him the next time he's here."

"Oh, darn." Paris snapped her fingers as she swung her hand through the air as if she was seriously disappointed. "Or I could not worry about the dress and wear what I have on for the graduation."

Wilfred looked her over in her all-black clothes and leather jacket and gave her a disapproving look. "You would be seriously under-dressed in that attire."

"I'd be comfortable and wouldn't throw up," Paris replied.

"I'm not sure why vomiting would be at risk," Wilfred said quite seriously, always the picture of matter-of-factness.

"I'm allergic to dresses," Paris remarked.

Many of the students gathered around snickered, entertained by Paris' continued dislike of the ball gown idea.

"I don't show any evidence that a person can be allergic to a style of clothing," Wilfred offered. "Are you quite certain that you have this allergy?"

Christine laughed beside Paris, having arrived after fixing her makeup from crying during Art of Love class. "She's joking, Wil. Paris doesn't like pretty things."

Paris batted her eyes at her friend. "I like you."

Pretending to blush, Christine smiled. "Oh, you're trying to butter me up, aren't you? It's Wil who you need to butter up so he doesn't make you wear the ball gown at the graduation ceremony."

"I think you're getting ahead of yourself with worry about the graduation ceremony to begin with," Becky said smugly. "You have exams to pass tomorrow, and if you don't, you'll be gone. Then there's finals and so many other requirements to pass."

"I know, right," Christine gushed, turning to Paris. "You have to rely on your brains to pass exams instead of coasting by on your family's money and reputation. And by reputation, I mean a bunch of socialites who make threats when they don't get what they want."

Becky stuck her hands on her hips, a look of offense heavy on her face. "How dare you. I earn my way the same as everyone else."

"Really?" Christine challenged. "Then what is the main secret ingredient in a magical fruit tart meant to create good communication between two romantic potentials?"

Becky's mouth slammed shut, obvious confusion on her face. "That's not going to be on the exam for Magical Cooking."

"So you don't know it," Christine spat with a sigh and folded her arms.

"How do you know what's going to be on the test?" Paris asked, remembering that Chef Ash didn't want to pony up any information on the subject.

"I know," Becky replied, turning her attention to Christine. "If I were you, I'd worry a lot less about what I know to pass my exams and a little more about how your family's reputation could affect your standing at the college. I hear your father lost yet another job."

Seemingly unaffected by the jab, Christine rolled her eyes. "He hated that job. Those with talent don't waste their time selling out for a buck. The Montgomerys wouldn't know anything about that since you all come with a price tag."

A loud gasp of protest spilled from Becky's mouth. Before she could voice her complaint, Wilfred held up his hand, halting the discussion.

"I think it's time we give focus to today's lesson. It will assist you all when it comes to the final ceremony, which I hope you all attend. There's no reason you all can't make it to completion since you've made it this far at the college."

"Well, some of us made it," Christine said from the corner of her mouth, although her mutter was loud enough for all to hear. "Some of us rode this far on coattails."

"Today," Wilfred continued over the giggles and chatter, "we'll be honing skills related to modeling."

"Oh, I'm really going to be sick now," Paris groaned.

Pretending he hadn't heard her, Wilfred went on. "You see, models know how to present themselves in a way that's not only pleasing to view but also shows off their attire while capitalizing on their best features. It is undoubtedly an art form and a skill."

"Yeah, so much skill," Paris joked, mostly to herself. "Walk, walk, walk. Pivot. Look. Walk, walk, walk. Talk about rocket science."

"Modeling," Wilfred cut in with a deliberate tone, "might look easy, but favorably presenting yourself is not. You must know how to master poise and grace and exude a charm that people can only capture with their eyes. Today we will take turns learning to walk with purpose and poise and present ourselves in captivating ways."

Paris had a slew of jokes to volley, but her heart wasn't in it, so she decided not to let them loose. Truthfully, something she'd never admit aloud was that she could somewhat appreciate the pageantry that went along with all this. There was something alluring about models and those who could present themselves in captivating ways.

She didn't know what use it served in the world, but she thought it could serve as art or inspiration, like the things she learned about in Art of Love. Paris hadn't forgotten the headmistress' words about staying open-minded. She felt there was something she could take away from this experience, even if it meant she had to wear a dress to do it.

Paris would deal with that last part when it got closer. First, she had to pass her exams to keep her spot at the college. Then she could breathe easier.

CHAPTER SIX

Chef Ash still wasn't giving away any information on his class or the exam at lunch. A grumpy mood replaced his usually easygoing demeanor and made him almost look like a different person.

Paris didn't know what had most at the college in a sour mood, but she was taking notes and going to figure it out. There were so many new things going on at Happily Ever After College that it was hard to know its cause. The exams around the corner naturally stressed some. Then there was a new tension that turned many emotional or on edge. Paris didn't know what to make of that.

She was about to pressure Chef Ash again for information when her phone buzzed in her pocket. Since it was in silent mode, that meant the message was from someone who could bypass the settings like Papa Creola or Mama Jamba.

However, when Paris retrieved her phone, she was surprised to find the message wasn't from either. To her shock and excitement, the text was from her mother, Liv. It was some of the coolest, most unexpected news.

The message read:

Your father and I are ready to reenter the world. Papa Creola is allowing it. We want to return to the House of Fourteen as Warriors. Will you please join us tonight as we shock the world who thinks we've been dead for fifteen years? We don't want to do this without you.

Her look of shock didn't go unnoticed by Christine, Chef Ash, Hemingway, and Penny. They all went silent for a moment.

"Okay, pony up." Christine motioned for Paris to spill it. "What's the message say?"

In reply, Paris pushed her phone across the table at her friend. Christine leaned over, as did the rest, reading the text message.

"Oh wow." Chef Ash looked up at Paris with awe.

"That's wonderful," Hemingway agreed.

"How exciting," Penny added.

"I want to go," Christine said in a conspiratorial whisper.

"You can't," Chef Ash informed her. "Only Royals like Paris and the Beaufonts can get into the House of Fourteen. That will be quite the experience. I hear that the Chamber of the Tree is amazing, with a light for each magician on the planet and so many oddities governed by magic as old as time itself."

"You *are* a romantic," Christine muttered with her chin on her hand. "How could I not want to go now after you sold it like that?"

"I'm sure that Paris will give us a full report," Hemingway offered. "That's wonderful that your parents won't be a secret anymore, and everyone will know they've returned."

"Yeah, and maybe your parents can kick Becky's parents' butts," Christine joked. "Then they'll think twice before sticking their nose in everyone's business."

"I think that those two back as Warriors will make a world of difference," Penny said in a low voice. "I heard that they had the biggest impact of anyone in the last hundred years, policing magic and keeping the demon population at bay."

"Where did you hear such things?" Christine challenged as she turned to Penny, appearing interested.

"People are always whispering about Liv and Stefan and how things aren't the same since they disappeared," Penny said shyly. "There are so many rumors about what happened to them. Wait until people find out they're back. It will restore hope in so many ways."

Paris gulped, disbelieving that they were talking about her parents. It was hard to fathom that her mother and father were these people of legend. Not only that, but they wanted her by their sides as they reentered the world. She was going to the House of Fourteen that night. She would be there beside her parents as they revealed they were still alive. Then she'd see as change started, marked by hope.

"Well, it appears that after tonight, the truth will come out." Paris felt a lump in her throat. "I'll no longer be an orphan. Everyone will know that my parents are back. They'll know the full story. And everything will change."

Hemingway gave her a hopeful look. "Everything will change for the better. This is the beginning of your new, more expansive life."

CHAPTER SEVEN

When Paris strode outside onto the Enchanted Grounds, alongside her friends, she was surprised by who she found standing on the lawn. Everyone seemed surprised.

"Holy guacamole!" Christine exclaimed at the sight before them.

"It's a real dragon!" another student gushed while rushing over to where the majestic blue dragon stood beside his rider.

Paris knew that her Aunt Sophia had access to enter Happily Ever After College and hoped that she'd visit soon but didn't know it would be then. She was thrilled to see her there and only wished that she could spend more time with her catching up, but she had Magical Gardening.

Since interested students were already politely mobbing the dragon and rider, Paris hung back for a moment beside Hemingway, who wore a coy expression. She gave him a pleading look. "I don't suppose you can let me out of today's lesson even though we have exams tomorrow and I'm sure we're reviewing?"

He shook his head. "First off, because your famous aunt shows up at the college with her dragon, you think I'll let you out of class?"

Paris flushed with shame. "Yeah, sorry. That's kind of a Becky move."

Hemingway laughed. "No, her family aren't nearly as cool and courageous. Second, we aren't reviewing for the exam. Everything you need to know on the multiple-choice test is in the textbook, which I think you've inhaled."

"Three times," Paris added.

He chuckled again. "Meanwhile, my fairy students are stuttering over the big words in the first section. I think you'll do fine on tomorrow's exam. It will cover the first few chapters."

Paris sighed with relief. "That's good news because now, with the thing tonight with my parents, I don't think I have time to study."

Hemingway nodded in understanding. "Yeah, but what else are you supposed to do? Tell your long-lost parents to postpone their reentry to the world because you have to learn to do the foxtrot?"

It did seem ridiculous, Paris had to admit. Her life was so strange. "Hopefully, I can eke by with a passable grade. It's funny that the only class I'm worried about at this point is ballroom dancing."

"Yeah, I think you'll ace your other courses, especially Magical Cooking, which I hear you excel at," Hemingway offered. "We can practice for ballroom dancing beforehand."

"Great, but you're not going to let me out of class briefly so I can catch up with my aunt who is visiting the college?" Paris asked in a hopeful voice, trying to catch sight of Sophia through the crowd of students.

"I would," Hemingway drew out the word with a sneaky grin, "but it might surprise you to learn that Sophia Beaufont isn't here to see you."

"What?" Paris was almost offended. "She said she'd come to the college to visit me soon."

"I'm sure she did." Hemingway rocked on his heels, still looking like he was holding onto a secret of sorts. "I invited her here today."

"You did?" Paris was surprised. "Why?"

"Well, I contacted the Dragon Elite, and I guess Hiker Wallace, their leader sent Sophia," Hemingway explained. "It makes sense since she has access to Happily Ever After College."

"Why did you contact them? What's going on?"

He pointed at the Bewilder Forest, which had regrown rapidly. Thanks to Paris' hybrid blood, it looked different than before. It wasn't as thick now, but in time, it should be as dense as before. The tree trunks were thin but tall with a silent promise that they would expand and take over the grounds soon. There were strange and enticing colors and smells and sounds emanating from the forest. Although it wasn't off-limits anymore, the headmistress had asked that the students not enter the Bewilder Forest yet.

Once it started to regrow, there were many new plants and things to classify. Hemingway had worried that too much traffic through the forest might stifle its growth. Soon after opening it to students, it had been closed. Paris couldn't wait to discover all the strange and magical things that were filling the new forest—all spawned from her halfling blood.

"I found something exciting in the Bewilder Forest that I thought might be of interest to the dragonriders," Hemingway explained. "So I contacted them, and they sent your aunt. I'm looking forward to meeting a real dragonrider, but more importantly, a Beaufont."

Paris was more than intrigued. There was something in the Bewilder Forest that would be of interest to the Dragon Elite. She had no idea what that could be, but she couldn't wait to find out.

She pointed at Sophia and Lunis, who were still getting tons of attention from the excited students. "It appears that everyone else is interested in meeting them too."

CHAPTER EIGHT

Sophia broke through the crowd at the sight of Paris and gracefully held her in an embrace—greeting her warmly.

"It's so nice to see you here," Sophia said when she pulled away, looking Paris over. "What a treat. I'm thrilled to have an excuse to see you in your element."

Without saying it, Paris knew that her aunt noticed the obvious differences between how she dressed in all black and the rest of the students in their blue gowns. All eyes were on the pair, not hiding their curiosity as the Beaufonts greeted each other.

"It's great to see you here too!" Paris realized that she was clasping Sophia's hands in hers, grateful to have a family member there. It made it feel real, as though she was truly a Beaufont and it wasn't all a rumor she'd told people at the college.

"What about me, Pare?" Lunis asked dryly, still crowded by students. "How great is it to see me? I'm kind of a big deal, you know."

Paris laughed, still not used to the idea that the timeless blue dragon had the silliest sense of humor. She expected that he would be serious, spouting great wisdom and being conservative in speech. The blue dragon was everything but serious.

"Lunis, it's fantastic to see you," she replied.

"You're a big deal, all right," Sophia volleyed at Lunis. "Like, a few thousand tons of junk food wrapped in dragon's hide."

"I think you're insinuating that I'm fat, Sophia." Lunis' snout was suddenly high in the air.

"How rude," one of the students remarked, patting Lunis thoughtfully.

"You're not fat," another student offered.

"Oh, no, I totally am," Lunis countered. "Sophia took a picture of me last Christmas, and it's still printing."

The group laughed. The students, like Paris originally, hadn't expected the blue dragon to make jokes—especially not bad ones.

"Well, it's a real treat to have you two here." Hemingway took the spot next to Paris and offered his hand to Sophia. "I'm Hemingway Noble, the one who contacted the Dragon Elite. It's nice to meet you."

There were many excited whispers from around the group of students.

"Nice to meet you, Hemingway. We were intrigued by your report. I'm excited to learn more."

"What's going on?" a student asked loudly.

"Oh! This is neat!" another student said to her friend.

Hemingway held up his hands, quieting the excited students. "As Headmistress Starr has urged you, we're still in preliminary stages of exploring and classifying the things in the Bewilder Forest and need your continued patience.

"Once we have a better grasp of the new life in the forest, we'll invite you all to explore and learn. It's important that we first get a handle on things and also ensure there's nothing that could be of harm to our students or anyone else. Most of what we're discovering in the Bewilder Forest are brand new species and require much research."

"Wow!" a student exclaimed, followed by many other enthusiastic comments.

Paris gulped, not as impassioned as the other students since she knew it was her blood creating new plants and more. She didn't know how all that was possible, but magic made many things happen that were unexplainable.

"Since you all have an exam tomorrow," Hemingway continued, "I'm going to ask that you all go to the greenhouse and study the textbook for the remainder of the class. There are no easy ways to pass the test. You must know the information."

With obvious disappointment, many of the students nodded before heading to the greenhouse. Many looked longingly over their shoulders at Lunis and Sophia, some waving as they trudged away, a bit deflated.

"Well, good luck with whatever you came here to see," Paris said to Sophia, trying to keep her disappointment out of her voice.

"Oh, you don't want to come along then?" Hemingway sported a sly grin, knowing she did.

Paris' eyes widened with surprise. "What? I can? Really?"

"Well, as we discussed, you already know the material on the exam," Hemingway stated. "Plus, the Bewilder Forest was regrown by your blood. So I think that if anyone gets a sneak peek, it should be you."

Paris was so thrilled that she didn't know what to say. She beamed at Hemingway and Sophia, grateful she could accompany them on this expedition. However, she was also aware of the tension deep in the pit of her stomach—nervous about what she'd find in the Bewilder Forest.

The brand-new place was a product of her: part magician, part fairy, with a little demon blood.

CHAPTER NINE

"Tonight?" Sophia asked Paris as the three strode toward the Bewilder Forest, Lunis bringing up the rear. "That's so exciting that Liv and Stefan are returning to the House. People are going to be shocked. What a sight that will be to see."

"I'm nervous," Paris admitted. "No one knows about me. So on top of the House learning that my parents are back, they'll learn about me."

"I can understand that," Sophia said sensitively. "It's a lot at once and seems like a lot of pressure, but don't worry. You're going to be a star when they reveal that you're a halfling." She looked out proudly at the Bewilder Forest. "I mean, look at what you're capable of creating."

"It is pretty incredible," Hemingway added, awe in his tone.

"Don't worry about having too much attention," Lunis offered. "Liv is pretty much a diva who will take center stage and not share the spotlight with anyone else."

Sophia rolled her eyes at her dragon. "That's not true. She has a commanding presence and speaks her mind freely. Stefan happens to be the strong, quiet type."

"So, what are you taking us to see?" Paris asked Hemingway, her excitement almost too much.

He flashed a sideways grin at her. "Don't you want to be surprised?"

"I've had a lifetime of surprises, but sure," she answered.

"That reminds me," Lunis began casually. "You know what my friend the custodian said when he jumped out of the closet?"

"You don't have a custodian friend," Sophia said dryly.

"What did he say?" Hemingway encouraged with an amused look.

"Supplies!" Lunis laughed.

Paris and Hemingway both laughed. Sophia shook her head, not looking impressed.

As they approached the Bewilder Forest, so many things competed for Paris' attention. Plants of all sizes, shapes, and colors filled the forest floor. Little eyes poked through thick leaves every so often. In the branches overhead were the strange songs of various unseen birds. The trees also appeared to be from another world with rainbow-colored trunks or unique textures or feather-like leaves. It truly felt as if Paris had stepped onto a different planet.

"Have you contacted Bermuda Laurens, the author of *Magical Creatures* and the utmost expert on animals?" Sophia asked Hemingway when they paused on the edge of the forest.

He shook his head. "It's on my list though. Thanks to your help, I have her contact information."

"She will be highly curious about all these new species," Sophia stated.

"Astrid, the plant expert on Roya Lane, is also interested in the things we're classifying," Hemingway explained.

"I can't believe that your blood grew all this," Sophia said to Paris, her eyes wide as she took in the sights around them. "You continue to astonish me."

Hemingway nodded proudly. "So far, I've cataloged sixty-five new species of plants. The animals aren't my specialty, but there are dozens I don't think can be found anywhere else."

"Oh, Bermuda is going to have a field day here!" Sophia said with excitement.

"What I think you'll find of supreme interest is that." Hemingway pointed ahead at something streaking through low branches, expertly maneuvering through the dense forest.

In the darkened area, it was hard for Paris to make out exactly what she saw at first. It appeared to be a flying insect of sorts, but there was more to it.

"Oh, wow," Sophia murmured.

"Talk about cool," Lunis added.

"What is it?" Paris narrowed her eyes at the creature. It was a beautiful bright blue dragonfly with a long body and wings to match. However, that wasn't what was so interesting. The bizarre part was sitting on the top of the dragonfly as it swerved around branches heading in their direction.

Sitting atop the large blue dragonfly was none other than the tiniest fairy Paris had ever seen.

Sophia grinned wide, nodding at her niece. "*That* is none other than the first dragonfly rider in history, sparked by your halfling blood."

CHAPTER TEN

"I want one," Lunis said with a dreamy expression, watching the dragonfly and rider zip through the air.

"I think they have to stay here," Hemingway explained diplomatically.

"You already have a menagerie of animals," Sophia scolded her dragon.

"I don't have a tiny fairy and a dragonfly that totally matches me," Lunis sang.

The blue dragonfly did match Lunis. It landed on the top of a large red mushroom as the tiny fairy pulled on what appeared to be thin vines fashioned into reins and a bridle. Once the dragonfly's wings settled still, the fairy slid out of the makeshift saddle and stood on top of the mushroom. It looked up at the three people and dragon and waved.

"It's adorable," Lunis said.

"It's a he," Sophia corrected.

She was right. The tiny fairy was about an inch tall and had light blue wings. He'd pulled his blond hair back in a low ponytail and wore clothes made from leaves and other materials from the Bewilder Forest.

"Can they talk?" Sophia asked Hemingway.

He nodded. "Problem is, I can't understand them."

"Oh, well, that makes sense," she replied. "I guess they'd have their own language."

"Not only that," Hemingway stated. "Watch." He leaned low. "Hey, how are you today?"

The tiny fairy opened his mouth and spoke quickly. His words didn't make sense to Paris and sounded like a series of squeaks.

"Seriously, that's adorable." Lunis looked as though he might fall over from cuteness overload.

"They're too tiny for us to hear them?" Paris questioned. "Maybe we can get a megaphone."

"Good idea," Hemingway said proudly, standing tall once more. "Yes, I think they speak their language, although they seem to understand what I say."

"How many are there?" Sophia asked. "Is this the only one who rides a dragonfly? I have so many questions. This is fascinating."

Hemingway looked ready to burst when he held up a single finger, pausing her. "This is the most exciting part. Hold on." He leaned down again, his nose inches from the small fairy and dragonfly. "Can you call the rest of your tribe? My friends would like to meet them."

The fairy flashed a toothy grin, tucking his thumbs into his armpits and nodding. He then put two fingers in his mouth and made a loud, high-pitched whistle.

At first, nothing happened. Paris scanned the forest around them, wondering what she was looking for. She glanced down at her feet, not daring to move, afraid that she might step on one of the miniature fairies.

However, the sound of hundreds of beating wings stole her attention seconds later. She tensed, worried that a swarm of bees or something dangerous could be heading in their direction.

Through the darkened forest, a few dozen dragonflies soared in their direction. Atop each one of them were little fairies of various colors—all of them matching their ride.

"Amazing." Sophia watched as the dragonfly riders zipped around them, seeming to put on a show for their new guests, squeaks echoing from their tiny mouths.

"I thought you'd appreciate this," Hemingway said, his eyes dazzled with amazement.

Lunis nodded. "It's an entire clan of fairy dragonfly riders."

Paris held her breath, watching as the swarm of dragonflies zoomed around them before retreating into the forest once more as if they only dared to make a brief appearance.

"They must have bonded with the dragonflies out of a mutual benefit," Sophia mused.

"They communicate with each other," Lunis added. "There are obvious similarities to us."

Sophia nodded, watching as the last of the dragonflies and riders disappeared. She glanced down at the lone fairy and blue dragonrider on the red mushroom. "You all are amazing."

The fairy bowed low, and when he straightened, he kissed his hand and blew it at Sophia as if to say, "You are too."

Turning to Paris, Hemingway looked at her with an expression that made her feel like a queen. "Do you see what you created? An entire world that's complex and amazing and full of so much love. This forest is like you, Paris, and I can't wait to explore it more."

CHAPTER ELEVEN

Paris wished that she could have spent the rest of the afternoon hanging out in the Bewilder Forest with Sophia, Lunis, and Hemingway. However, the dragon and his rider had a meeting at the White House—which impressed Hemingway. He was, of course, grateful that they stopped by to see his discovery with the dragonfly riders, although there wasn't anything to do about them except appreciate the fact that they existed.

Even if Sophia and Lunis could have hung around Happily Ever After College, Paris had to go to Magical Cooking. First off, she wanted to find out what was wrong with Chef Ash. Also, she needed to prepare for the exam the next day. She wasn't worried about passing the test, whether it was a multiple-choice exam or cooking assignment, but it was the responsible thing to at least know what she needed to prepare for.

When Paris cruised into the magical cooking classroom, she immediately halted. Standing at the front of the demonstration kitchen was a woman in the traditional blue gown and pink sash that showed she was a graduate fairy godmother. Paris didn't recognize her. However, she instantly didn't like her and didn't know exactly why.

Maybe it was the pinched expression on the woman's face as she scrutinized every student as they took their seat. Perhaps it was because she had a familiar look about her that Paris couldn't quite place but definitely didn't like. Or maybe it was because she was tapping her slippered foot impatiently as Paris stood inside the classroom.

"Take a seat, Miss Beaufont," the woman said in a clipped tone. She had her long grayish hair tied up into a tight bun, and her wrinkled hands pressed together in front of her. "I'm about to start class."

"Where's Chef Ash?" Paris didn't move from her spot.

"Over here, Paris." He raised his hand at a nearby workstation.

Paris looked between Chef Ash and the woman. "What are you doing over there?" she asked him and glanced at the fairy godmother. "Who are you?"

"Chef Ash isn't and has never been qualified to teach magical cooking," the woman explained in a snooty tone. "Once it came to the FGA board that classes were being taught by those who aren't fairy godmother graduates, new assignments were made."

"I thought the board could only make recommendations." Paris looked between Chef Ash and the woman, wanting this to all be some stupid mistake.

"Miss Beaufont, the FGA board can unfortunately only make recommendations about curriculum under the current Saint Valentine," the fairy godmother explained rudely. "However, classes must be taught by accredited teachers, or Happily Ever After College risks losing its reputation and much more. Enrollment is abysmally low already, and now I see why."

"Mother, Magical Gardening is taught by the groundskeeper," Becky Montgomery said from her workstation.

Mother. With that thought, Paris put it all together. Of course, Becky's mother had stuck her nose into the college's business and was now going to try and ruin things there.

The woman coughed with disapproval heavy in her tone. "I am aware, Rebecca. Thank you. We are currently looking for a fairy godmother suitable to take over that class and ballroom dancing. The help shouldn't teach classes. That's disgraceful. Thankfully for you all, I'm a culinary expert and had an opening in my schedule to take over this class for you."

"Hemingway and Wilfred are more than qualified to teach their classes and don't need to be replaced," Paris said in an angry rush. "Chef Ash is also a culinary expert who we are lucky to have as a professor."

Chef Ash shot her a grateful smile from his place at a workstation.

"It seems that your lack of qualified instructors has lowered your expectations, Miss Beaufont," the woman said. "The cook who makes the students' meals shouldn't be the one to teach the classes. Saint Valentine and the headmistress have ignored some boundaries at the college for too long. Although the board can't at the current time change curriculum, when it comes to qualified instructors, we have much authority."

"Chef Ash is more than a cook who scrambles eggs." Paris felt heat rise to her face. She was about ready to boil the fairy godmother before her.

"The fact that you, Chef Ash, serve savory dishes as options to the students has also come to the board's attention," the woman said to him with a pointed look. "You are aware that fairies operate best when given a diet of desserts."

"Not all fairies do," Chef Ash countered. "Some prefer a wide range, and although sweets are good at restoring magic quickly, a balanced diet does have a benefit."

The woman sighed, shaking her head. "There are so many misconceptions for me to fix, it seems."

"So now the board is going to tell us what we can eat?" Paris questioned. "Anything else? You want to tell us what position to sleep in? Maybe how many times we chew our food? Oh, how about how to tie our shoes."

The fairy godmother narrowed her gaze on Paris' black combat boots. "I think we'd like to start by telling you what to wear and that shoes with laces have no place in a fairy godmother's closet."

"Wow, you really need a hobby," Paris jabbed. "You have way too much time on your hands if you're sticking your nose into my closet or eating habits."

"Do you see what I mean, Mother?" Becky said in a shrill voice.

The woman nodded. "I do, indeed, Rebecca." She glanced around the room with an annoyed expression. "Now, take your seat, Miss Beaufont. I've granted you way too much time speaking out of turn in this class. It won't happen again."

Instead of replying or taking her usual seat, Paris strode straight over to where Chef Ash was sitting and pulled up a stool and sat next to him. He seemed surprised by her allegiance, but she winked at him and smiled.

"Hey, I'll be copying off you," she said loud enough for others to hear. "Can't go wrong looking over the expert's shoulder."

This produced gasps and whispers from around the classroom. Becky's mother appeared about ready to throw a knife at Paris. Instead, she clapped her wrinkled hands together.

"Now, I'm Virginia Montgomery, and I'll be your instructor for Magical Cooking from now on. Unfortunately, I haven't been here to assist in your success for tomorrow's exam. That means many of you probably won't do very well on the test, and as you know, a failing grade could mean your expulsion from Happily Ever After College."

She sighed and shrugged as if this was unfortunate, but her hands were tied in the matter. "That's simply the way it is, and the FGA board hopes to avoid such problems for students in the future. However, you will have today to work on the project I'll assign you for tomorrow's exam. It isn't much time and will undoubtedly prove problematic for some."

Virginia looked straight at Paris, threat heavy in her gaze.

So that's the game she's playing. They were going to try and get rid of her this way. Still, Paris knew how to cook, so she wasn't that worried.

However, at that precise moment, Virginia Montgomery flashed a victorious smile as if she knew what Paris was thinking. "For your exam, you have to make something so sweet that it wows me visually so much that without trying it, I can taste the sugar. Only real fairies can pass this test!"

CHAPTER TWELVE

If Paris wasn't worried before, the look that Chef Ash gave her didn't fill her with confidence. She wanted to assure the guy sitting beside her that she was up for this challenge, as though he was the one who needed the confidence boost and not her. However, she knew that he was worried for a good reason. Virginia Montgomery was up to something, and it was definitely about getting Paris kicked out of Happily Ever After College.

Picking up a metal whisk, the fairy godmother swished it through the air with a triumphant expression. A lacy tablecloth covering an assortment of dishes on the workstation behind her disappeared, presenting several plates. Everything was bright and colorful and full of sugar.

"Here we have some superb examples of what I'm looking for," Virginia said proudly, looking at the dishes. She pointed with the wand of sorts to the first dish. "I've made fairy bread. It's an Australian tradition loved by children and adults alike."

"Isn't it white bread with butter and covered in sprinkles?" Paris asked, looking at the slices of bread coated in bright little balls of every color.

"It's whimsical and pleasing to the eye to look at," Virginia countered.

"There's no way that can taste good," Paris challenged.

Beside her, Chef Ash nodded in agreement. "Not to mention there isn't much skill involved in making it."

"I know, I expect more from the Australians," Christine joked from another workstation.

"The taste of a dish should be second to how it looks," Virginia said, her chest puffed out and chin held high in the air.

"I think you're living in a reversed world," Paris teased. "Are you sure you're supposed to be on Earth? Maybe you should check with Mother Nature, and you're supposed to be on another planet."

Virginia huffed. "Don't be absurd. We eat with our eyes and therefore food needs to look visually pleasing, similar to a fairy. We present ourselves in a way that looks appealing so others know we're sweet before interacting with us."

"It so happens that appearances can be deceptive," Paris said under her breath to Chef Ash, but loud enough for others to hear.

"Other options for you all to make," Virginia went on in a terse voice, indicating a tall pink cake on the workstation, "would be a rosewater cake with lavender frosting, covered in fondant and stenciled with gold leaf—"

"There's no way that can taste good," Paris interrupted before she could stop herself.

"Miss Beaufont, do you make it a habit of interjecting your opinion throughout every single class?" Virginia asked as if she was interested in Paris' answer.

However, before she could reply, Becky said, "She does, and it really interferes with the learning experience."

"Your closed mind and lack of brain cells are what interferes with the learning experience," Christine cut in boldly.

"Miss Welsh, I don't feel that you're in any position to make criticisms about others at the college," Virginia asserted with threat laced into her tone.

"Why is that?" Christine fired back.

"I hear that your standing at the college is under careful consideration," she replied smugly.

"Oh, is it because my father is under investigation after being let go from his job?" Christine dared to ask boldly, not backing down from the challenge or looking the least bit shameful.

The response threw Virginia off momentarily, her eyes flicking around the room before returning to Christine. "It has and always will be the standard of Happily Ever After College to educate students who have good conduct, as well as come from families with such records."

"He's a scapegoat," Christine argued, her face flushing red. "It shouldn't matter anyway. I earned my entrance into this college, and I'll earn my diploma. I bet it really burns you up that Headmistress Starr has allowed people like me in here and created scholarships that allow others who aren't rich to become fairy godmothers. If it were up to the Montgomerys, only the rich and elite would be here."

Paris' gaze drifted to Penny Pullman, who she knew was only at Happily Ever After College because of a scholarship. If the current board got their way, not only would many of the faculty change, but many of the enrollment standards. Paris knew that she had to help Saint Valentine overthrow the board's rule before they got too powerful. It appeared that even with Agent Ruby gone, there were still problems running rampant at FGA. No doubt, it resulted from the modern ways challenging tradition, which the old stuffy families didn't want to let go of.

"Those with money and status are proving that they meet critical standards," Virginia argued, not put off by Christine's argument. "For too long, those in power at the college and FGA have confused these ideals, believing that they're unimportant indicators of worth. Soon, we'll reinstate tradition, and those who prove themselves suitable will fill our ranks. Those who do not, well, you all can find yourself a spot at Tooth Fairy College."

"It's pretty entertaining that you're not even trying to mask your crusty old thinking and prejudice." Paris rolled her eyes at the fairy godmother.

"As for you, Miss Beaufont." Virginia settled her gaze on her. "A student whose guardian was found impersonating a fairy and wrongly filling the position of a detective for FLEA has no business talking out of turn or at all at this college."

Whispers filled the room at Paris' back, but she ignored them, knowing the truth about Uncle John would come out sooner rather than later.

"My uncle was posing as a fairy for a good reason," Paris argued with confidence. "His cover was blown when he was trying to apprehend a criminal who worked at FGA as an agent. Probably one of your good buddies who subscribes to your notions about elitism. Do you know where Agent Ruby is? He's probably staying at your guest cottage, right?"

Virginia huffed in offense as many students stifled laughs or gasps of shock. "There is no reason for a mortal to pose as a fairy. Again, the actions of a family really do reflect on our students and should be criteria for enrollment or dismissal."

Paris faked a yawn as though she was bored with the conversation. "Really? Because my uncle was trying to keep me alive from a deadly danger in my parents' absence. I think the Montgomerys would throw their young to the wolves if it meant saving their elders' butts."

The fairy godmother's eyes widened with shock and offense. Paris knew she was punching low, but the woman had asked for it, insulting all her friends. If she wanted to box, she was going to get knocked out.

"It was rather unfortunate that your parents abandoned you," Virginia stated. "Again, it's a reason that we must demand only families of noble status become fairy godmothers."

"Paris is a Royal for the House of Fourteen," Chef Ash countered with an angry expression.

"She's also an orphan with a criminal record." Virginia didn't look deterred.

"I'm not, actually." Paris hid a grin. "My parents didn't abandon me. They risked everything to keep me alive. And they happen to be back."

At this admission, excited whispers broke out around the room.

Paris heard her parent's names repeated over and over again behind her. She knew it wasn't her place to reveal such things, but the House of Fourteen would know in a few hours, and it would spread fast. What was the harm in telling the class then? Especially because it put a severely sour expression on Virginia's face.

"Liv Beaufont and Stefan Ludwig are back?" the fairy godmother asked.

Paris nodded. "Yes, and in a few hours, they'll be taking their places once more as Warriors for the House of Fourteen."

"Which is pretty much one of the highest-ranking positions on the globe," Chef Ash said with a wide grin.

"So if we're worried about Paris passing your test for family status and wealth, Mrs. Montgomery, I think she has," Christine sang. "The Beaufonts outrank your family on every single metric."

Virginia *harrumphed*, offense heavy on her wrinkled face. "We've wasted enough class time with this discussion. You all will get to work on your desserts now. Regardless of status, students can still be dismissed from Happily Ever After College if they fail exams."

CHAPTER THIRTEEN

As Paris suspected, the rosewater cake didn't taste good. Virginia Montgomery had required that all the students taste it as she sliced pieces for the class. The idea was to taste the sweetness before even taking a bite based on the appearance of the pink cake covered in thick fondant and gold leaf.

"It's overdone." Paris pushed the crumbs around on her plate.

Chef Ash nodded. "Yes, less is more often with desserts. People love making masterpieces out of cakes, but the construction process turns it dry and inedible. A good baker knows how to preserve the integrity of the ingredients while also creating something visually pleasing. It's a balancing act."

Paris sighed. "We both know that desserts aren't my strong suit. Not with the standards that Snooty McSnottison is using."

"I know." Chef Ash looked around the room as students stirred their ingredients or poured cake batter into pans. "You have a mastery of magical ingredients and your foods taste excellent, but presentation isn't your strong suit. What did you make for today?"

Paris' dessert was already in the oven. She'd finished it and stuck it in while Chef Ash was consoling Christine, who was more affected by the insults Virginia had volleyed at her than she previously had let on in front of the class.

"Well, since berries are ripe in the garden, I decided to make a cobbler." Paris grabbed the oven mitts. "Since it's supposed to taste sweet before you even take a bite, I used infectious sugar as a magical ingredient."

She pulled the tray of mixed berry cobbler from the oven, steam rising from it. The smell wafted from the dessert, making many students turn around, their eyes wide and mouths watering.

"Very smart idea, indeed," Chef Ash commented, smacking his lips as if he couldn't wait to take a bite. "I can already taste the sweetness."

"It looks abominable," Virginia said over Paris' shoulder.

She rolled her eyes, realizing she should have sensed the soulless demon lurking nearby. "It's a cobbler. They're supposed to look wholesome and taste like summer."

"The assignment was to make a dessert that looks so visually pleasing that you can taste the sweetness before you take a bite," Virginia argued.

"You can taste the sweetness." Chef Ash waved to bring the aroma lent from the infectious sugar to his nose.

"That's because Miss Beaufont cheated, using magical ingredients instead of making something that looks appealing." Virginia narrowed her eyes at her, looking her up and down. "That's typical of a magician. They refuse to follow the rules and know nothing of appearance."

"We know how to think for ourselves," Paris said through clenched teeth, her patience waning. "You said to make it so you could taste the sweetness before taking a bite. I figured out a way to do that. You physically can taste it. If I did it based on appearance, you would have subjectively said that it didn't look sweet enough based on how it looked. I don't see how you can grade me when your standards are so arbitrary."

Virginia flashed a victorious smile. "Yet, I'm the instructor, and my grade is what matters. Good luck with tomorrow's exams, Miss Beaufont. It appears you're going to need it."

The fairy godmother's blue gown swished behind her as she swept from the workstation, her nose held in the air.

Tension suddenly filled Paris' chest. She hadn't worried about passing the Magical Cooking exam until right then. Students had to pass all their exams along the way at the college to keep their enrollment. Paris didn't know what she'd do if she failed. Being a fairy godmother was all she wanted…surprisingly.

"Don't worry," Chef Ash whispered, reading the tension on her face. "I'm going to help you pass the exam tomorrow. You're going to make a dessert that looks so delicious and beautiful that it will give that witch a cavity."

CHAPTER FOURTEEN

Paris' worries about passing her exams were as far away from her mind as Happily Ever College was when she stepped through the portal to Santa Monica. She was pretty sure that Faraday would want to tour the House of Fourteen with her on that occasion, always fascinated by new magical places. However, when Paris went to her room to fetch him, he was nowhere to be found. She reasoned that she would bring him the next time. As a Royal, she should always be able to get into the place.

Her nerves jittered around in her chest as she stood on the boardwalk in Santa Monica, searching for her parents. It was their first trip out of the Fantastical Armory since returning to this dimension. They'd told her to meet them in that spot, and they'd go to the House of Fourteen together.

The last and only time that Paris was in Santa Monica was with Faraday. The squirrel had said that according to his research, the House of Fourteen was in a rundown palm reading shop. On that occasion, Paris had tried to enter, but the locked door prevented her. Then the Deathly Shadow came after her, and she never got into the House of Fourteen.

She stood in front of the seemingly abandoned palm reading

shop, blinking at it in confusion. On one side of it was a taqueria. The other was a souvenir shop. All around, clogging up the boardwalk were hipsters who were too cool for school, teenagers wearing short-shorts and backward caps, and confused tourists with selfie sticks.

It was hard for Paris to believe that inside the small two-story palm reading shop was the most powerful governing organization for magical beings. It proved that appearances were deceiving. The fact that it was in such a prominent location in Santa Monica, right off the Pacific Ocean, was also intriguing.

She grimaced at the sand all around the boardwalk, hoping that she didn't get any in her boots. Paris didn't do sand. She also didn't do tourist locations, palm-reading shops, or crowds. It appeared that she'd have to swallow her pride on that this time and any others when she visited the House of Fourteen.

"Oh, I forgot how much I loathed Santa Monica," her mother's voice said at Paris' back. She turned to find her parents closing a portal behind them.

Stefan nodded, looking around. "In fifteen years, nothing has really changed."

"No, the hippies seem to have gotten dirtier," Liv argued, looking around at the crowd before she found Paris standing nearby. She rushed over, threw her arms around her shoulders, and pulled her in tightly. "Oh, good, you found the location. I hope you didn't talk to any strangers."

Paris laughed, pulled away, and hugged her father. "Don't worry. I can handle myself."

"I know you can," Liv replied. "It's just that talking to the hippies down here will kill brain cells. If you make eye contact with the tourists, they'll ask for directions. If you even glance at a hipster, they'll pull their giant sunglasses down their nose, hoping you mistake them for a celebrity."

Stefan shook his head, looking at his daughter. "Liv doesn't have a tolerance for what she calls the shabby chic West Coasters."

Paris nodded and glanced around. "I can see why." She then ran her gaze over her parents. "So you're ready to come back? How do you feel?"

"Like kicking some ass," Liv replied. "Hanging out in Papa's basement for the last several weeks was enough to make me go insane."

Stefan agreed with a nod. "Yeah, I get that we had to assimilate, but another day locked away, and I think I would've lost my mind."

"You want me with you for this?" Paris indicated the palm reading shop. "Are you sure? It seems as though there will be a lot you have to explain at once."

"Oh, I can't wait to see the shocked faces of the Warriors and Councilors." Liv rubbed her hands together. "Regardless, our sudden appearance is going to require a lot of explaining. It's better if we can show you off to help others understand. Most didn't even know you were born, and no one knew you were a halfling. I think you'll get more attention than us at this reunion."

"I'm not sure I like that," Paris admitted.

Her mother shrugged. "Well, I'm afraid you'll have to get over it. You can't be a one-of-a-kind halfling and not expect others to regard you as exceptional."

"Don't worry," Stefan consoled. "The news about you being at Happily Ever After College has undoubtedly spread, so others will be aware of you. But seeing you, well, I'm afraid some might stare."

Turning to face the palm reading shop, Liv looked up at it.

"This place also hasn't changed a single bit, has it."

"So this is the location of the House of Fourteen?" Paris questioned. "I tried to get in there once when I was looking for information about you two and couldn't. Are you sure I can?'

Stefan nodded. "For sure, you can. It's just that you have to know how."

"Oh, does it involve a spell?" Paris asked.

Liv shook her head. "No, it's a palm reading shop." She held up her hand. "So it needs to read your palm to know that you're a Royal."

She strode forward, her hand extended. She paused in front of a single black door with a hand-painted sign that read "Closed." Around the door was a black and red checkered frame, and above it, a neon sign flashed "Palm Readings."

The building, which was narrow and seemingly connected to the ones around it, had one window on the second story covered by a set of paisley drapes, with various shadows moving behind it.

Liv pressed her hand to the spot under the surface as her gaze went to the gold door handle. A moment later, it glowed briefly before the door swung back, showing only blackness on the other side and a strange musty smell spilling out to the boardwalk.

She glanced over her shoulder at Paris. "The door will shut behind me. Go through next, and your father will wait on the other side. You have to enter on your own, but I promise, it doesn't hurt a bit."

Paris nodded, a lump in her throat.

Probably sensing her nervousness about entering a new world, Liv flashed her a smile. "Get ready to meet your ancestry. What you're about to see is your birthright if you ever want it."

CHAPTER FIFTEEN

When the door to the palm reading shop closed behind Liv, Paris looked back at her father. He gave her an encouraging nod.

"Your mother is the queen of making an exit," he offered with a laugh. "But she's right. The House of Fourteen is your birthright. I know you're feeling a lot of pressure, and I'm not going to take it away by telling you that you're extra special in regard to being a Royal."

Paris gulped. "I'm afraid to ask how."

He chuckled again. "Well, before Liv started making changes in the House, it was illegal for two Royals to marry and have children. The old Councilors were afraid that by allowing such things, it would muddy the bloodlines and the structure of the House would fall apart. However, Liv pushed for change and for things to evolve."

"Because you two wanted to be together," Paris guessed.

"Because your mother won't rest until the world is the very best it can be," Stefan answered. "She's the only person I've ever met who isn't afraid of change. She's always pushing things to be better. Before Liv, mortals couldn't see magic, and every magician's magic was registered, observed, and scrutinized.

"Before your mother, the Mortal Seven were as long-lost as the

Forgotten Archives, which told the history that many didn't want anyone to remember. After Liv, mortals and other magical races were invited into the House of Fourteen to vote in major decisions. We formed alliances with the giants, elves, and gnomes for the first time in history."

"She also changed it so Royals could marry," Paris added, guessing again.

"She lobbied so Royals could marry whoever they wanted," Stefan corrected. "Before, Royals were only allowed to create unions with other magicians."

"Because again they were worried about muddying bloodlines," Paris stated, thinking that the old Councilors for the House of Fourteen seemed as backward and rigid as the FGA board.

"That's right," Stefan confirmed. "Fae and magicians can't breed. Nor can magicians with any other race or vice-versa for the most part. So if Royals were marrying outside their race, well, it was only a matter of time before the families died out.

"Liv, during a time of radical change, capitalized on all that she'd done for the House of Fourteen, saving magic and the Forgotten Archives. She used that momentum to convince the Council to allow Royals to marry whoever they wanted. Since they created alliances with the other races, they couldn't very well restrict such things."

"Yeah, that would have been hypocritical," Paris agreed.

"When the Council allowed Royals to marry outside their race, well, they finally accepted that we could also marry each other," Stefan said proudly. "We were married the very next month. I would have married that woman no matter what, but not having to hide our relationship was a gift."

"So, if you two were the first Royals to marry, then..." Paris stopped speaking, the implications of what her father was telling her coming to light.

"You, as far as I'm aware, are the first Royal offspring from two House families," Stefan continued, echoing her thoughts. "You're the only magician and fairy halfling, with demon blood, and also the blood of two Royal families. You're extraordinary by anyone's standards."

Paris didn't feel very extraordinary, learning this knowledge. Her gaze fell to the ground, not really seeing anything—her thoughts ran through her head at a maddening pace.

Stefan gently rested his hand on his daughter's shoulder, bringing her eyes up to meet his. "That's who you happen to be. I know you didn't ask for it. Although who you are might be incredible, what impresses me is who you chose to be, which is a brave and talented person with an exceptional heart. When you walk through that door, know that we made you special, but you always get the choice about who you are."

CHAPTER SIXTEEN

In a few moments, Paris' father had told her something that overwhelmed her, followed by something that made her feel soaring hope. It was a lot to know that she was so unique. The pressure, when she overthought it, was crushing. However, her father was right. At the end of the day, Paris got to decide who she was and what she did with the power given to her—and that felt right and less intimidating.

Without another word, feeling much more confident than before, Paris laid her hand on the palm reading shop's door, as her mother had. When the gold handle glowed, Paris pushed the door back, holding her breath as she stepped into the House of the Fourteen for the first time.

"It's about time," Liv said when Paris stepped through into a darkened corridor. The sunlight from Santa Monica lit the area briefly before the door shut, casting them in mostly darkness again as Paris' eyes worked to adjust to the dim lighting. "I assumed your father took you to get ice cream and abandoned me."

Paris laughed and looked around, taking in what little she could see of her surroundings. "He was telling me that I'm the first with Royal blood from two different families."

Liv nodded. "The Beaufonts are one of the two remaining founding families, hence the reason you carry that name."

"Yeah, since there's only you, Clark, and Sophia, I guess there was a concern of losing the Beaufont name," Paris remarked.

Liv sighed. "Yeah, and we can't count on Clark to have some offspring, I'm assuming."

"So what will happen to the Beaufonts?" Paris asked.

"Well, I'm not going anywhere any time soon, so it's not a worry," Liv explained. "I'm sure in time, Sophia will have children. You might too if you decide. The Beaufont name will continue."

Stefan stepped through the door, casting them in sunlight for a moment, making Paris squint from the brightness. When the door closed behind him, Paris took another look around.

The entryway wasn't what she'd expected to find at the front of the rundown palm reading shop. Although it was dark, light from a long hallway was enough for Paris to make out the round entryway.

There were large white statues on pedestals along the walls. It was hard to make out the marble floor under her feet. The large chandelier hanging overhead was unlit.

The only light was from flame-lit torches in the long corridor ahead. The entire wide hallway was gold—the walls, floor, and the strange writing on the glistening walls.

"Again, some things haven't changed." Liv looked down the hallway, the same as Paris.

Stefan agreed. "Yeah, for as much as the House of Fourteen changed over the years, no one did much with the interior design."

"If it looks the same after all this time," Liv began, "that probably means not much has changed for the House of Fourteen."

Liv caught the confused expression on Paris' face and offered a caring smile. "The House of Fourteen changes based on who resides within, what's going on with the Council and Warriors, and other factors. It's more like an organic living being than an actual structure."

"That's fascinating," Paris said in awe.

"It can be unless it gets in a mood and decides to lock you out of certain rooms or sequester you to the library," Liv muttered. "It used to do that type of thing to me all the time when I was younger, trying to discipline me for my bad attitude."

Stefan laughed, looking at Paris. "I know you're shocked that your mother ever had a bad attitude. Also, don't go into the library on the top floor if you're confused, lost, or otherwise not feeling your best."

"It's best not to go to the library unless you're with someone else," Liv corrected. "The buddy system works best when you're visiting that library."

"Why is that?" Paris questioned.

"Because it's a fickle little place that likes to play games with readers," Liv answered. "If you enter it, searching for answers or a certain book, you'll probably find yourself lost for ages."

"The library directs your paths based on your thoughts," Stefan continued to explain. "So if you're unsure what you're looking for, you won't find it. You have to use your thoughts to guide you to find books." He glanced at his wife with a look of affection. "Remember when I found you sleeping in the library with a duffle bag of kittens and a giant sword?"

She nodded, smiling with fond memories in her eyes. "Yeah, what were you looking for when you found me?"

"Strangely enough, I had been on the search for a humorous volume—something that would make me laugh." He chuckled, his eyes dancing with delight. "I found it."

"Why did you have a bag of kittens?" Paris asked.

"I was cat-sitting for Rory," Liv stated. "I have the worst and best friends."

"That wasn't as amusing as when I found your mother by the fountain in the garden." Stefan nudged Paris' arm with his while staring at Liv. "She was passed out after being attacked by a mermaid. Lying beside her was a cold, wet, dead woman."

"Oh, good times." Liv laughed.

"On that occasion, I asked Liv why she was hanging out in such a precarious state," Stefan explained. "Her answer: 'Because I have the worst friends.'"

"I think I need a lot more information for that story to make sense," Paris admitted, thoroughly amused by her parents' stories.

"That time, it was because I was doing a favor for King Rudolf Sweetwater," Liv imparted. "That dead girl went on to be his wife."

"Wow, that's not how I guessed that story would end," Paris remarked.

"It never is with King Rudolf," Stefan related before giving his daughter a serious look. "So I wonder, what do you see when you look out at the House of Fourteen?"

She blinked at him. "I'm guessing the same as you. White statues. Marble floors. Gold hallways. Strange writing."

Stefan glanced fondly at his wife. "Pretty close."

"It must be because she's a fairy godmother in training," Liv said to him. "Sophia could see things in the House once she joined the dragonriders."

"Again, I'm not following you two," Paris interjected.

Stefan nodded understandingly. "Warriors and Councilors can see different things in the House of Fourteen that other Royals can't." He stepped forward and waved at the wall of strange symbols. It danced under his fingers, rearranging and twirling around. "We can even read the Founders' language now. Most don't see the symbols, or the corridor looks completely different."

Liv nodded. "Even most Royals can't enter the Chamber of the Tree where the Council and Warriors meet. I checked with Clark, and you'll be able to enter, either because he pulled strings or because you're you and full of special sauce. Either way, you'll get in."

"The House of Fourteen is amazing." Paris looked around in awe of the place.

"It really is," Liv agreed. She grabbed her daughter's hand and tugged her forward. "You haven't even seen the coolest part yet."

CHAPTER SEVENTEEN

Liv led her daughter to the far end of the corridor, where it split. On the left side was a large door. On the right was a small door, but it was far more interesting than the one across from it.

"What is that?" Paris looked at the reflective surface that moved like water in front of her.

"That's the Door of Reflection," Stefan explained, arriving at Paris' shoulder. "All Warriors and Councilors must pass through it each time we meet. It's like entering your worst nightmare, serving up your greatest fears for you to face and fight before a meeting."

"That sounds awful," Paris nearly stuttered.

Liv nodded. "It definitely sucks. The idea is that it cleanses us of worries beforehand so we're strong and ready to face the real world dangers out there."

Stefan gave his wife an intense look. "I've learned, through my many times walking through the Door of Reflection, that my mind can come up with worse fears than exist in the real world."

"So once you've faced that in the Door of Reflection, reality is easy then?" Paris questioned.

He nodded with a dimpled grin. "Exactly."

Paris stiffened, wondering what the Door of Reflection would serve up to her. Probably something to do with getting kicked out of Happily Ever After College or disappointing her parents or losing Uncle John now that he was being forced into the mortal world again. Now that she was considering her greatest fears, there was a myriad of possibilities.

"Don't worry." Liv settled a comforting hand on her shoulder from beside her. "You shouldn't have to pass through the Door of Reflection the same as us. It's only ever been Warriors and Councilors. Even Sophia, when she's visited the Chamber of the Tree on dragonrider business, didn't have to pass through it the same way. You aren't working for the House of Fourteen. You're a visitor and will only have to face it if you elect to become a Warrior or a Councilor one day."

Paris nodded, relief flooding her chest. "You two have to pass through it in a moment?"

They both agreed with small nods.

"It's supposed to be good for us," Stefan repeated, invoking confidence in his words.

"Like a good deep teeth-cleaning," Liv added with a grin. "I'll go first. I think the meeting started, like, ten minutes ago, so we're arriving fashionably late. Just my style."

Stefan grinned too. "Oh, I can't wait to see the faces of the Council when we waltz in there."

"Then it will get even better when we unveil our reason for slacking on the job," Liv sang, looking back at her daughter. "Our greatest treasure. And the person I assume will soon be treasured by many."

Paris' mother gave her a pure look of love before stepping through the Door of Reflection and disappearing once more.

Stefan also gave Paris a look of encouragement before following his wife into the Chamber of the Tree.

Left alone in the darkened corridor, Paris knew that it was her turn to step through into the place of magicians and to finally claim her title as a Beaufont, a halfling, as one with demon blood. As a Royal.

CHAPTER EIGHTEEN

Glancing over her shoulder, Paris got the feeling that something was watching her. She remembered that the House of Fourteen was seemingly alive and guessed that it had eyes of sorts and probably was. Who knew how it would react based on her arrival? Maybe it would be like the Bewilder Forest and produce new plants or creatures.

Realizing that she was stalling, Paris faced forward. She reasoned that on the other side of the Door of Reflection, there would be gasps and shock from those who didn't know that Liv and Stefan were alive. Sucking in a breath, Paris stepped through the rippling surface of the Door of Reflection.

At first, she thought it had prevented her from entering the Chamber of the Tree because the reflective surface felt exactly like stepping through water, pushing her back. However, her intention drove her forward, carrying her to the other side.

No nightmarish visions gripped her the way Liv described the Door of Reflection working. Instead, she entered a room with a domed ceiling. Thousands of twinkling lights covered it, representing magicians all over the world.

The Warriors for the House of Fourteen stood in a half-circle, dressed similarly to Liv and Stefan in combat clothes with weapons strapped to their sides or across their backs. The Councilors formed the other half of the circle. They sat on a high bench at the back of the room, looking down at the Warriors.

Then she noticed that the half-circle of the Council table and the one where the Warriors stoically stood matched the chamber's shape.

On the far wall, behind the Council, was a picture of a giant tree. Its trunk was gold, and each of the seven branches swept overhead and forked in two directions. One part of each branch glowed blue, while the other was bright green.

Paris squinted and noticed that the branches showed the family surnames of the Seven: DeVries, Ludwig, Beaufont, Martinez, Mantovani, Takahashi, and Rosario. Each colored portion held the name of the Councilor or Warrior. The last one had the green section of the branch lit up, and under it was Clark's name. The blue said Alicia.

On either side of the bench were two other creatures who belonged to no one. Paris had heard about them. A large white tiger stood on one side and a small black crow on the other. According to her parents, the animals represented truth and lies. Good and evil. Yin and yang. Jude was the tiger, and Diabolos was the crow. They both glanced at Paris when she stepped forward.

The Warriors all turned to face her, and the Councilors regarded her with confusion as she stepped out of the shadows and into the room's light.

"Who are you?" a Japanese man with a bald head and a black goatee asked from the bench.

Paris saw the few familiar faces she knew on the council: Hester DeVries, Raina Ludwig, and Clark Beaufont. She swallowed, grateful when her mother flashed her a confident nod, encouraging her.

"My name is Paris Beaufont." She tried to keep the nervousness out of her voice.

Many of the Councilors and Warriors gasped in surprise. All eyes were on Paris, studying her with gripping curiosity. Her gaze flew back and forth between her parents.

"A new Beaufont?" a Spanish man with black curly hair said from the Council seats.

Apparently, news from Happily Ever After College hadn't spread to the House of Fourteen. Liv had mentioned this as a possibility since they tended to stay somewhat separate. Father Time had also been working to quiet the rumors about Paris, especially those connecting her to demon blood. He said it would be best if Stefan confronted that subject straight-on first.

"She's our daughter," Liv said proudly, indicating her and Stefan.

"Is that where you've been?" a man with a thick French accent asked, also from the Council seats.

Liv waved Paris forward to join her where she stood in the center of the circle. "No, unfortunately, Stefan and I spent the last fifteen years not watching our daughter grow up. We were stuck in another dimension, and while many years passed in this world, we were only gone for a day."

"Is that why you don't appear to have aged?" the French man asked.

Liv nodded and pointed at the guy. "That's GiGi Mantovani. You can hardly understand a word he says, but he's a lot less snooty than the Councilor he replaced," she said to Paris, helping her out with names. "Yes, time moved very differently in the world where we got stuck."

"How did you get there?" the Japanese guy questioned.

"Haro Takahashi," Liv supplied. "He's pretty all right and one of the two remaining founding families."

"Are you going to insert your opinion on each person here?" the Spanish man asked.

"Armando Rosario," Liv said, looking at Paris. "He totally has zero sense of humor, and his votes are usually pretty self-serving." She then flashed a grin at the Councilor and nodded. "Yes, I'm educating my daughter, giving her a crash course on the House of Fourteen."

Stefan stifled a laugh and stepped forward. "Our daughter was born twenty years ago. Most weren't aware of it because right before her birth, it came to light that her fate was tied to the Deathly Shadow."

"She's the girl the prophecy was about?" Hester DeVries leaned forward, and the light caught her short gray hair.

Paris had met her at the reunion party at her parents' place. She was a healer. Her sister Trudy, the Warrior, was a seer, but no one knew that. Most didn't know that she was the one who made the prophecy that involved the Deathly Shadow and Paris. Even in the magical world, people shunned seers because their powers were scary.

"Yes, that's correct," Stefan answered.

"Then that would mean…" Haro's voice faded, his eyes wide.

Whispers filled the Chamber of the Tree.

Liv nodded with confidence. "Yes, the prophecy stated that the Deathly Shadow would need to absorb the power of a halfling that was part-magician and part-fairy to return to form and take over. Paris is the first and only halfling of that combination and the one the prophecy referred to."

CHAPTER NINETEEN

Haro Takahashi bolted to a standing position, his hands pressed to the bench as he stared down intently at Paris. "She is the halfling?"

She froze, aware that everyone was studying her. Paris knew a prophecy involved her, but she didn't realize that so many people knew about it and were waiting for the halfling to come along. She guessed that she should have, in hindsight. The Deathly Shadow was a big deal and a force that many wanted gone.

The Warriors had all turned to face her. Paris recognized Alicia, who was smiling at her politely. Besides her parents, Alicia was the only Warrior she knew. However, standing in front of her Aunt Raina was a large man with a thick beard and kind eyes. She guessed he was Fane Popa-Ludwig—the leader of the original werewolf pack in Lupei who married her aunt to preserve her father's position as Warrior.

"Yes, Paris is half-fairy and half-magician," Stefan answered when many of the murmurs had died away.

"How?" an older woman with gray and black hair asked from the Council.

"That's Fantasia Martinez," Liv said over her shoulder to Paris. "She makes fantastic tamales but also seems to always vote the way

Armando Rosario tells her to. I believe the two families are in cahoots."

"We are not," Armando Rosario argued at once.

"You've been gone for fifteen years," Fantasia Martinez said, her tone clipped. "It would be unwise to think you know how things run here, Olivia."

"I go by Liv, and even after fifteen years, you damn well know that."

Clark cleared his throat, leaning forward on the bench. "Paris became half-fairy based on a wish that Liv made on a genie's lamp when she was pregnant."

That caused many to gasp in shock.

"A genie's lamp!" someone exclaimed.

"That's very risky!" another yelled.

"But why?"

Stefan sighed. "My wife did this to protect our unborn child from inheriting a potential problem from me."

"A disease?" Haro Takahashi asked.

Stefan shook his head. "No, many years ago, before Paris was born, I was bitten by a demon."

"What!" a nearby Warrior exclaimed, stepping away from Stefan as if he might attack her.

"It's true," he admitted. "But I'm fine. Liv helped to cure me, but the blood of the demon will always be inside me."

"You really should have made this information known to the Council," Gigi Mantovani said sternly.

"At that time," Liv began, "the Council was much more corrupt than it is now."

"It isn't corrupt now," Fantasia said in an offended tone.

"We'll see," Liv sang. "My point is that if Stefan had told the Council that a demon had bitten him, they would have kicked him out of his place."

"Well, of course," Armando Rosario said at once. "It's common knowledge that those bitten by demons are irrational and prone to rage. A Warrior can't be such things."

"Actually, since most are never cured of demonism before it takes over, there is little information on the subject," Liv refuted. "What you're spouting is conjecture. Stefan is one of very few who was bitten and cured before demonism set in, so there's little information on the subject."

"From what I know," Hester DeVries began in a small voice, "those cured will always carry the blood of the demon. They won't ever turn, but it does influence their behavior."

"See there!" Armando Rosario accused, pointing down at Stefan.

"As I was saying," Hester continued, pursing her lips at the other Councilor. "The demon blood, once cured, makes the person vehemently repulsed by evil. They have an unyielding desire to stamp out what they almost became. Not only that, but they're excellent at tracking demons, able to find the monsters since they possess their blood and all their skills."

"So you have all the power, strength, and longevity of a demon but also the drive to end them," Haro Takahashi guessed.

Stefan nodded. "Which is what makes me an excellent demon hunter."

"Unfortunately," Hester continued. "A drawback is that Stefan can pass on his demon blood."

"Which was why you made the wish on the genie's lamp," Haro Takahashi assumed, looking at Liv.

"Yes, and the crafty little jerk made our daughter a halfling when I asked that she not become a demon," Liv explained.

"You, like your father, still have the blood of the demon," Raina stated rather than asked.

"That's right." Paris' voice sounded strange in the large chamber when she finally spoke among the large audience.

"So you're a halfling with demon blood." Haro shook his head. "Fascinating."

"Like me," Stefan began, "her demon component makes her repulsed by evil and driven to fight it. Her half-fairy part counters it."

"That makes sense," Hester stated.

"Although fairies otherwise would be very susceptible to demons," Haro added.

"Yes, but a fairy can't be turned into a demon, unlike a magician," Clark offered.

"Where have you been, Paris Beaufont?" Armando Rosario asked. "Why are we only now learning of you?"

Before she could reply, thankfully, her mother jumped in.

"After hearing the prophecy," Liv began, "we hid Paris away, knowing the Deathly Shadow wanted her. However, it soon became apparent we would need to face that evil and end it. However, he opened a vortex to another dimension and locked us away. Knowing that Paris needed to remain safe, my and Stefan's family worked to hide her on Roya Lane and raised her there."

"No House of Fourteen members were allowed there until recently," Haro stated, musing on the information.

"Because Papa Creola knew that things had to remain secret to keep Paris and everything else safe," Stefan answered. "When she was ready, he helped to prepare her to bring us back since she was the only one who could." He looked at her with deep fondness. "Our daughter successfully defeated the Deathly Shadow, put him in a container, opened the vortex to the world where we were stuck, and brought us back."

"Wow," a Warrior nearby said in hushed amazement.

Many others regarded her with awe and shock.

"You sound like you'll make quite the Warrior one day." Haro appeared impressed.

"She would," Liv chirped. "But she has her sights set on something better. Instead of only fighting injustice, our daughter will bring love to the world. Paris is studying to become a fairy godmother."

CHAPTER TWENTY

"That's why we haven't heard anything about you," Gigi Mantovani said from the Council bench.

"Yes, Happily Ever After and FGA remain quite separate from our world," Hester DeVries stated.

"I had heard rumor of a halfling," Fantasia Martinez admitted. "But I thought it was impossible."

"And I had heard something about someone with demon blood," Armando Rosario offered.

"Yes, I thought I heard Stefan's name mentioned in connection," Fantasia added.

"Since we assumed that you and Liv were dead, we paid it no notice," Haro said, his brown eyes dancing with curiosity. "This is a fascinating revelation."

"I think you're overlooking the fact that they kept us in the dark and orchestrated much behind our backs." Armando sounded offended.

"You were kept in the dark because if the Deathly Shadow found our daughter, he would have killed her and come into full power," Liv said through gritted teeth.

"Then we would have had an evil on our hands that no one could defeat." Clark stared down the bench at the other Councilor.

"So, you and Alicia," Armando fired. "Are you even married?"

"Of course," Alicia answered shrilly.

"Only for show, I bet," Fantasia stated. "Because there aren't any other Beaufonts."

"Or Ludwigs," GiGi added.

"When Liv and Stefan went missing, you all orchestrated things so you didn't lose your positions in the House, is that right?" Armando accused.

"Raina and I are madly in love," Fane admitted, his voice deep.

A smile flickered to Paris' mouth. The werewolf wasn't lying. She knew that from her parents. Raina and Fane had married because he'd agreed to take Stefan's position as Warrior when he went missing. Although they weren't in love initially and married out of necessity, like Clark and Alicia, they'd fallen for each other over the last fifteen years—much unlike her other aunt and uncle.

"It isn't our job or business to question the relationships in the House of Fourteen," Hester stated. "A Beaufont and a Ludwig legally filled the positions, and that's all that counts."

"But the lies," Armando protested.

"Were told to hide and protect a young halfling," Trudy DeVries interjected from the far side of the Chamber of the Tree. She was tall and had short hair like her sister and the same kind eyes.

"Now we have back the best Warrior the House of Fourteen has ever known," another Warrior said beside Liv, giving her a fond look.

"Thanks, Emilio." Liv leaned in Paris' direction. "He's a Mantovani and married to a fae because he's not as closed-minded as the rest of his family."

Some laughed at this. GiGi Mantovani wasn't one of them.

"We also have back the best demon hunter," a woman said beside Stefan. She had a long black braid down her back and a sword strapped to her hip.

"Thank you, Shika." Stefan saluted the other Warrior.

"That's Shika Takahashi," Liv said to Paris. "Their family is good through and through, although Haro is always a swing vote."

There was another community chuckle at this.

"It doesn't matter that Liv and Stefan are back." Armando sighed. "Their positions are filled."

"Actually, I would like to return to my magitech business," Alicia cut in. "If Liv is willing to take my position as Warrior, that is."

Liv smiled wide. "Sure, I guess I can take that off your hands, but you need to help me get cable programming of shows from the last fifteen years. I have so many *Great British Baking Show* seasons to catch up on."

"If Stefan wants my position as Warrior, I don't mind stepping down too," Fane offered. "My pack could use my help, although I do plan to stay here in Los Angeles for the most part." He gave his wife Raina a thoughtful look, which she returned.

"That isn't how things work," Fantasia objected in a disapproving tone.

"I'm fine with it," Hester stated.

"I say we put it to a vote," Clark offered.

"All those in favor of Liv and Stefan taking their positions as Warriors back?" Raina asked.

Hester, Clark, Raina, and Haro all raised their hands, muttering yes.

"Then it's decided, and Liv and Stefan are back with the House of Fourteen!" Clark exclaimed with a rare note of excitement in his voice.

Stefan stepped even with his wife, putting his arm around her. "It's good to be back."

"Well, technically for us, we weren't really gone," Liv joked. "Can I get a day off? I need to catch up on laundry."

Many laughed at this.

"We could desperately use both of your help." Hester was suddenly quite serious. "There are many problems that fall under your expertise, and we all fear that things are about to get incredibly out of control soon."

CHAPTER TWENTY-ONE

"What's going on?" Liv asked. "I bet there's a surplus of nacho cheese in my absence."

"Probably," Hester said with a good-natured look. "The giants have refused to update their treaty. You, Warrior Beaufont, were the only one they would work with. Since you've been gone, they've fallen out of the alliance."

Liv threw her hands up and rolled her eyes. "Seriously, do you know how long it took me to get them to sign that?"

"I know," Hester agreed.

"We sent Fane, but that only made things worse," Clark stated.

Fane gave Liv a look of apology. "I'm sorry. I don't know where things went wrong, but they kicked me off the island straight away."

"Probably because they think werewolves are demons," Liv stated. "For as big a brain as you'd think giants would have, they can be pretty dumb on certain subjects."

"Yes, and after that, they wouldn't listen to anyone else," Raina explained.

"No, because they probably think Fane has bitten all the other Warriors," Liv admitted. "Don't worry. I'll get the alliance back. Bermuda Laurens owes me a few dozen favors and will help. Her patience for me will be much higher since I haven't annoyed her in fifteen years."

"Without the alliance, there's been a domino effect of other problems," Haro stated. "Communication with the elves has faltered. No one seems to be able to make sense of reports from the fae."

"That's because you all don't speak Rudolf Sweetwater," Liv explained. "To understand what that man is saying, you have to inhale a bunch of helium and hold your breath until you're about to pass out."

"So you think you can restore relations, then?" Raina sounded hopeful.

"For sure," Liv stated. "I bet the gnomes have been having a field day without being policed on Roya Lane."

Many of the Councilors nodded.

"Yes, and it then trickles over into other magical law enforcement problems," Haro imparted. "Illegal contraband is on the rise, dangerous magical artifacts are turning up everywhere, and criminal activity is soon to be out of control."

"Although we've tried to get a handle on things, we couldn't secure the deals that you did," Trudy offered.

"I don't even know how you did it," Shika admitted.

"We took you for granted, for sure," Emilio added.

"With Warrior Beaufont back, she can focus on what she does best, striking deals and using strategy with the other races," Hester stated. "The rest of you can do what you do best and police magic. We were overwhelmed before."

"Then there's the demon problem," Clark flatly stated.

"Demon problem?" Stefan questioned. "What's going on?"

Hester frowned. "Well, to put it simply, they're out of control."

"None of us were very effective at hunting them," a man with dark hair and long sideburns said on the other side of Shika.

"That's Carlos Martinez," Liv informed Paris, still offering her input on all the strangers around her. "He's more humble than his cousin, Fantasia, but doesn't make as good tamales."

Carlos bowed to her.

"Now we know why we weren't as successful," another Warrior added.

"That's Maria Rosario," Liv explained to her daughter. "She's a good fighter but has a few screws loose if you know what I mean."

"I can hear you," Maria said dryly.

"And she has excellent hearing," Liv added with a laugh.

"Stefan was a great demon hunter before being bitten," Raina argued. "But yes, now he has advantages that make him even better."

"So the demon population needs to be cleaned up." Stefan puffed out his chest. "I can do that."

"It's not only that they're overrunning cities," Emilio Mantovani explained. "We've been getting reports that they're attacking fairies."

Stefan scratched his head. "Fairies? Strong wards that keep demons out usually protect them. How is it possible they're a target?"

"We don't know," Trudy answered. "There have been several reports from fairies stating that they're suffering from symptoms related to being leeched by demons. We're not sure when it's happening. Maybe when they're traveling between secure locations or something."

"I'll look into it immediately," Stefan said with confidence.

Haro sighed, looking relieved. "It seems as though many problems that have been plaguing us will soon disappear. I hope so, at least.

"It's good to have you two back." Hester looked between Liv and Stefan. "When you disappeared, we were all devastated. Without you fighting for justice and protecting the magical world, we've all suffered."

Liv, still with Stefan's arm around her, lifted her arm and laid it across Paris' shoulder. "That's nice to hear. Once we had our family back together and safe, we were happy to return to the world."

Hester smiled at Paris. "It's an honor to meet you, Paris Beaufont. You must know that you're one of a kind."

She nodded. "Yes, because I'm a halfling."

"With demon blood," Raina added.

"And the first offspring of two Royals," Clark stated.

"Yes, all that," Hester agreed. "But I think she's one of a kind because she's the daughter of Liv and Stefan, two of the most extraordinary people I've ever met."

CHAPTER TWENTY-TWO

"I can't believe you went to the House of Fourteen without me," Faraday complained as he pawed through a magazine.

"Well, you weren't around when I was leaving." Paris wished she didn't look so tired, but her schedule hadn't been conducive for much sleep.

"Wilfred had me picking out countertops for the workspaces for the lab the headmistress is having built for me," Faraday explained while turning another page of the magazine, which was full of chemistry tools and supplies. "I went with a neutral gray. I think you'll really like it."

"You know how I get about countertops," Paris teased. "Gray, talk about a showstopper color. Do you think you'll be able to focus with that much color seeking your attention?"

He batted his long eyelashes at her, not appearing amused. "It's a good canvas. That's the point."

"You're a squirrel who does science projects, not Van Gogh," Paris remarked, patting the skin under her eyes, trying to make herself look more awake.

"It's Van Gogh," he corrected, saying the last word as if he was coughing, making a sharp "f" sound.

"Sure, whatever you say," Paris teased. "I think that if a van can go, then Van Gogh does too."

Faraday cringed. "Please stop saying his name like that. It's common knowledge that it's pronounced Van Gogh."

"I love it when I debate common knowledge with a talking squirrel," Paris deadpanned, turning away from her vanity mirror—giving up on the cause of making herself look more awake. "Also, you should take something for that cough."

"What?" Faraday looked up suddenly, confused. "I don't have a cough… Oh, you mean… Very funny."

"Anyway, I'll take you on the next adventure I have to make up for you missing out on the House of Fourteen." Paris headed for the door. The sun wasn't even fully risen over the Enchanted Grounds of Happily Ever After College. "For right now, I have to go brush up on my foxtrot and practice making something that looks and tastes delicious."

"Make a cheesecake," Faraday offered. "Everyone loves a cheesecake."

"You love it because you're the strangest squirrel in the world."

"I am not," he argued, feigning offense as he glanced back down at his magazine. "Real quick before you leave, do you think I should go with a color-coded or photographic periodic table?"

Paris rolled her eyes and opened the door to her room. "Climb a tree, squirrel. That's what you should do."

He shivered again while turning another page of the magazine. "No, thanks. I'll hold off on the periodic table until we've had time to discuss it more. It isn't a decision to rush."

"You're so weird," Paris sang, heading out into the hallway and for the ballroom downstairs to meet Hemingway to practice. She couldn't believe that her fate at Happily Ever After College depended on dancing and baking, but Paris would do whatever it took to keep her place there. With all the options she had laid before her, all she wanted was to become a fairy godmother.

<h1 style="text-align:center">CHAPTER TWENTY-THREE</h1>

Unfortunately, Paris wouldn't know the results of her exams immediately. It was standard for the instructors to have some time to grade. However, on top of that, many of them and the students had suddenly fallen ill. It was a strange illness, Hemingway had explained at dinner that night as he and Paris dined on the patio.

Since no one knew what the cause was or if it was contagious, the students had been encouraged not to congregate in large groups.

"Classes are all suspended until the headmistress knows more," Hemingway explained, pushing his salad around but not looking all that hungry to eat the leafy greens.

"Yeah, there weren't that many students in most of my exams." Paris looked out on the grounds as the setting sun made the grassy lawn glisten.

He nodded. "Which is another reason for the delayed results, until everyone can sit for their exams."

"Or dance," Paris joked. Hemingway had helped her that morning, and she felt better about her performance in front of Wilfred than if she hadn't practiced. Whether it was enough to pass, she'd have to wait to find out, although the butler had looked somewhat impressed.

However, when Paris presented a chocolate cheesecake with raspberry compote and edible flowers to Virginia Montgomery, the fairy godmother's expression didn't give anything away. Chef Ash had said that if he were grading, she would have gotten top marks, but unfortunately for her, he wasn't and she'd have to wait to find out how she did.

"Are you worried about being replaced?" Paris asked Hemingway, sensing his worry.

"As an instructor?" he asked. "Yeah, although they've delayed making replacements due to this mystery illness. They aren't allowing any new instructors until we know what's causing people to get sick."

"It's weird, isn't it?" Paris remarked. "I mean, Christine said that she feels lethargic and depressed. Penny too. It's not a common illness. How do you feel?"

Hemingway shrugged, pushing his plate away. "I'm fine. You?"

Paris yawned, having been going all day and still running on fumes. "I'm good. I'm tired, but that's because I had little sleep and I've been stressing about my exams."

"You'll pass," he encouraged, smiling at her across the table.

"I don't know," Paris argued, looking out at the Bewilder Forest, noticing how much it had changed in a day or so. "Virginia Meany-Face has it out for me. The Montgomerys won't be happy until they've turned this place back into a socialite club. They think they're superior to everyone else, and it drives me crazy."

"Good." He drank some mint lemonade. "I like that about you."

Paris blushed, taking a drink too to cover her expression. "I don't get why people like them think they're so much better than everyone else."

"You know what the famous Hemingway said on the matter?" He flashed a sideways smile.

"Tell me," she encouraged.

"There is nothing noble in being superior to your fellow man; true nobility is being superior to your former self."

Paris smiled. "I like that. And I appreciate that you, Mr. Hemingway Noble, quote the other Hemingway on the subject of nobility. There's a nice symmetry to the whole thing."

He bowed his head. "Why, thank you, Ms. Paris Beaufont."

"Don't worry," she offered. "Headmistress Starr won't let you go. No one can teach your class better than you. I think she's struggling with the board breathing down her neck."

He nodded. "Yes, I think Willow is picking her battles right now. Emotions are heightened with so many not feeling themselves suddenly. I hope that we get to the bottom of whatever is causing it. Seeing so many like this is bizarre when they're all usually so happy and full of energy."

Paris was about to agree when her phone buzzed in her pocket. Since only people like Papa Creola could override silent mode on her phone, she decided to retrieve it. When she saw who it was, she knew she had to take the call.

CHAPTER TWENTY-FOUR

"Sorry, I have to take this." Paris gave Hemingway an apologetic look as she held up her ringing phone. "It's my dad."

He nodded understandingly. "When your long-lost father calls, you take it no matter what. Really, I think if your dad calls at all you're supposed to answer it."

Paris smiled at him. "Hey, Dad," she said into the phone, realizing how weird and right it felt to call him that.

"Hey, Pare," Stefan replied. "I'm sorry to bother you. I know you had exams today. How did they go?"

There was another strange thing. Paris was hanging out on the deserted grounds of Happily Ever After College having a phone call with her dad, who thoughtfully asked about her exams. "They went fine, I think. I won't know the results for a while. There's been an outbreak of an illness here."

"Are you okay?" Stefan asked in a rush.

"Yeah, I feel fine," she admitted, watching as Hemingway pretended not to listen, making another attempt at eating his salad.

"I figured you would be okay," Stefan said over the phone.

"Really? Why?" Paris wondered if he'd called about her exams. That did seem like a father thing to do. Uncle John had sent her a series of encouraging text messages that day, which was very thoughtful since he was facing so much turmoil after being kicked off Roya Lane. He said he was fine and happy to return to the real world, but Paris knew that it would be a big change for him. She was planning on checking on him now that she'd finished her exams.

"I think I know what's causing the fairies at the college to be ill," Stefan began. "It's a problem the Council was talking about. I think you have a demon infestation there at the college."

"What?" Paris exclaimed suddenly, making Hemingway's eyes jerk up to meet her frantic expression. She mouthed the word "demon" to clue him in immediately.

His eyes widened in shock.

"Yeah, I tracked a source that's around FGA headquarters," Stefan stated. "I can't get into the building though, because of its heavy wards against outsiders. That's usually how the fairies keep demons out because they're a huge energy source to demons—like a Thanksgiving dinner of emotions.

"Before, I thought that demons were leeching fairies when in transit, but even then, they usually have protective wards. Demons of fifteen years ago, when I was hunting them, didn't bother with fairies. They'd given up and fueled themselves on mortals mostly. However, something seems to have changed."

"How could a demon get in here?" Paris questioned. "Or FGA headquarters?"

"That's what I need to find out, but eradicating them is the first step," Stefan answered.

"If we have a demon hanging out here, leeching the fairies, shouldn't I be able to sense it?" Paris questioned.

"Yes, but you've been stressed about your exams," Stefan stated. "You might have read any extra emotions as being related to that."

Paris nodded, also thinking that the excitement and stress of her parents returning to the House of Fourteen would have overshadowed any emotion related to a neighboring demon. "If there is a demon here, how are we not seeing it?"

"They're masters of hiding," Stefan stated. "Most don't see them because they don't want to. Mortals especially don't see what they don't want to be real. Fairies too. I need to get in there to investigate."

"I can open a portal for you," Paris offered, but Hemingway shook his head immediately.

"You can't," Stefan said over the phone. "One must be invited to enter Happily Ever After College."

"I brought Faraday in here," she argued.

"He's a squirrel," her father replied. "I tried to speak with Saint Valentine, but due to the recent murder attempts and Agent Ruby being at large, he's refusing to talk to anyone. He's understandably paranoid now that Matters of the Heart, FGA, and Happily Ever After College are all plagued by a mysterious illness."

"Well, that's stupid," Paris spat. "You're trying to help."

Stefan sighed. "I know, but you have to realize that fairies and FGA specifically have operated very separately from the rest of the magical world. They don't like magicians much, thinking that we're cold and calculated, rather than emotional and all warm, fuzzy feelings."

"Well, I'll talk to Headmistress Starr and get you an invitation," Paris stated. "She's reasonable and respects magicians."

She glanced at Hemingway, sharing his secret about being a magician, which only she, Willow, and Mae Ling knew.

"Thank you," Stefan stated with a sigh of relief. "I was hoping you could help."

"Willow will be very grateful that you've found the cause of the illness," Paris stated. "With you on the job, the demons will be eradicated in no time."

"I appreciate that." Paris heard the smile in his voice. "I hope that it will be easy, but someone let demons into FGA and Happily Ever After College, which is my bigger concern. I can't get in there, so whoever did it, well, they're the real problem."

"Agent Ruby," Paris said with a sudden realization. "Of course, it has to be him."

"I would agree," Stefan stated. "Which means he's probably lurking somewhere around there, so you need to be careful. I suspect he wants revenge since you linked him to the murders of Agent Topaz and Agent Opal."

"Right." Paris gulped as she looked around the Enchanted Grounds. They didn't appear as warm and inviting as they had moments prior. The Bewilder Forest loomed with a dark, ominous presence.

"Of course, you need to be careful about the infestation you have at the college," Stefan continued. "I don't know that there's a demon there, but I tracked one to FGA headquarters, and the symptoms of the fairies suggest you do."

"I feel fine though," Paris stated. "Both Hemingway, my friend who is with me now, and I seem okay."

He glanced at her with a smile in his eyes at the mention of him being a friend rather than an instructor.

"Is Hemingway a fairy?" Stefan asked boldly.

"Well…" Paris didn't want to divulge his secret but was unable to lie to her dad.

"He's a magician, isn't he?" Stefan questioned.

"Yeah," she admitted, giving Hemingway a look of apology, although he didn't know she'd revealed his secret.

"Demons can't leech magicians the same as fairies," her father explained. "Your demon blood makes it so your fairy side wouldn't be affected."

"Oh, that's good news." Paris tilted the phone to the side to talk to Hemingway. "You and I are protected in a way from demons leeching us."

He nodded, filling in the rest that it was because they were magicians.

"However," Stefan said, an edge to his voice. "There's a bigger danger for your magician friend. Only we can turn into demons. If he gets bitten, the odds of him surviving it and not turning are small—you know that, Pare."

She nodded, gulped, and averted her eyes from Hemingway.

"I'd suggest that Hemingway leave the college until I get there and hunt down this demon," Stefan continued. "If he's the only magician amid fairies, he'll be too tantalizing for the demon to resist. They leech emotions to get stronger, and their main desire is to spread demonism. The one you have there is feasting, and it's only a matter of time before it's so strong that it will give me a run for my money before I get there to take it out."

"Okay," Paris said, still unable to look at Hemingway. She knew the last thing he'd want would be to leave Happily Ever After College. He had only gone a few times in his entire life, and it had always been with her. This was his home, and he was desperately attached to it.

"I'll get you an invitation to Happily Ever After College and FGA," Paris continued over the phone. "Then you can do what you do best and hunt down these demons."

"Thanks." Stefan laughed. "What I do best is loving and protecting my family, and that's what I'm going to do first. Be careful, Pare."

CHAPTER TWENTY-FIVE

"Demons." Headmistress Starr's head was leaning on her hand, and her face was pale. She didn't look like herself.

"It makes perfect sense." Mae Ling sat in her usual chair in the headmistress' office. She didn't look as bad as Willow, slumped behind her desk, but she wasn't faring very well.

Paris nodded, giving Hemingway a look beside her. She'd asked him to leave right away, explaining what her father had told her. He agreed but said that he couldn't leave until he knew that a solution was in the works. Paris sensed that he was stalling, not knowing where to go, not having spent much time outside the college.

"My father, Stefan Ludwig, can hunt the demons down and get rid of them," Paris continued. "The problem is that he can't get in here or FGA. He tried to contact Saint Valentine but was unable to. He needs an invitation."

Willow glanced at the love meter, which was dangerously low, yet again. "I wish I could help, but honestly, I don't think I can. Our magic as fairies is low, and as you can see, that's affecting love worldwide."

Mae Ling drew in a breath. "Fairies aren't able to create matches due to this sickness that's befallen us. No one is working. We can't."

"We have to get you out of here," Paris encouraged. "Can you send a message to Saint Valentine?"

Willow shook her head. "As you said, he can't be reached. He's gone into hiding, knowing that Agent Ruby is out there."

"But his fairies are under attack," Paris stated, her voice rising.

"Clearing us out of the college and FGA might not help," Mae Ling pointed out. "That might be what Agent Ruby wants and will put fairies in even more danger. We don't know what we're facing. There's nowhere for us to go that's safe."

"If you stay here, the demon will leech you, and the love meter will further plummet," Paris argued, livid that the fairies were accepting this. This was one of their shortcomings. They didn't react well when faced with danger. They didn't have the same self-preservation as magicians in that regard.

"The only solution is to get rid of the demons," Willow said slowly, the effort of talking seeming to cost her greatly.

"Well, to do that, my father needs to get in here and FGA," Paris stated.

"Again, I'm sorry, but I can't help you," Willow replied. "The magic it would cost me to invite Stefan here, and FGA and Matters of the Heart is simply too much."

"Then you leave here, restore your magic, and give him the invitation," Paris offered, desperately trying to find a solution.

"I'm afraid that by that time, it would be too late," Willow stated. "I can't leave the college. I will make an announcement to the students and staff and send a message to FGA. If any want to return to their homes, they can, although Mae Ling is right and that might be a part of the trap. Outside the college, there aren't the same protections as here."

"The protections aren't working." Paris vibrated with anger. "Agent Ruby has obviously figured out a way around them."

"Which is why I fear that we don't have any safe options," Mae Ling said, not sounding like her usual confident self.

"My father!" Paris exclaimed, now really mad. "He's your option. He needs an invitation!"

"There is a fairy who can grant him one here and FGA and Matters of the Heart," Willow began. "The two are located in the same building but the security to get into Matters of the Heart is different. This fairy, she would be the only one to get him into all three, as I can't grant invitations to anywhere but the college."

"Good! Great!" Paris said in a rush. "Where is this fairy? She's not here or at FGA being leeched, is she?"

Willow slowly shook her head, making Paris crazy with impatience. "No, Tiffer doesn't reside at any of the main locations. She has always remained off the grid."

"Where? Where can I find this Tiffer?" Paris questioned quickly, wanting to snap her fingers.

"I'm sorry, I don't know," Willow replied as if talking through a mouthful of molasses.

Paris' eyes bulged. "Are you serious?"

"Tiffer is one of the most powerful fairies, which is why she can grant you an invitation to all three locations," Mae Ling explained. "But in being so powerful, she prefers not to be easily found."

"Where do I look?" Paris questioned.

"I would recommend asking the person who supposedly saw her last," Willow answered.

"And that is?" Hemingway grew as impatient as Paris with this conversation.

"According to my memory, the last time someone saw Tiffer, she was dining with a man at a very prominent restaurant in Las Vegas." Mae Ling scratched her head, trying to think of the name.

"Vegas, man, great. Who is it?" Paris snapped her fingers.

"It was none other than the king of the fae," Willow answered. "That's why it made so much news. But finding him to ask about Tiffer's whereabouts might be difficult."

Paris rolled her eyes, realizing she should have seen this coming. "King Rudolf Sweetwater?"

"Yes, that's right," Willow affirmed.

Paris smiled, finally feeling on the verge of making progress. "Yeah, finding Uncle Ru won't be hard. The difficult part will be getting him to focus long enough to give me a straight answer."

CHAPTER TWENTY-SIX

A little reluctantly, Hemingway agreed to leave the college, but only because he was with Paris. She knew it was difficult for him to see the fairies so depleted, but he was in more danger than them.

The demons would continue to leech the fairies, slowly stealing their magic and making them depressed. According to her father, when Paris phoned him with an update, the demons would leech the fairies, stealing their energy and emotions. It wouldn't want to kill them, stealing all their reserves, because then it would have nothing left to leech.

That meant the fairies would trudge along at the college like sad zombies, hardly able to accomplish much. Thankfully, Wilfred as a magitech AI was unaffected by the demons and had taken over cooking from Chef Ash. All the fairies had to do was feed themselves, and they would survive. However, seeing them zapped was heartbreaking, and Paris desperately wanted to help them to recover. She had to find Uncle Rudolf, track down Tiffer, get an invitation for her father and allow him to do what he did best and kill some demons.

Easy, peasy, Paris thought as she and Hemingway stepped through a portal to Roya Lane, leaving Happily Ever After College behind.

"Our apartment is right up here." Paris pointed at a narrow staircase between two buildings.

"Are you sure it's okay if I stay in your uncle's and your place?" Hemingway looked around at all the curious sights on Roya Lane.

She nodded adamantly. "He's not there and can't be on Roya Lane anymore. And I'm obviously not going to be there."

"It can't be safe for you to be at the college," he argued as they marched up the stairs.

A wave of nostalgia washed over Paris as she neared the modest apartment where she'd grown up most of her life with Uncle John. "I'm the only one besides Wilfred who is safe there."

"You're part magician," Hemingway countered.

"Who has demon blood. They can't turn me because technically, I'm already one of them. That blood, according to my father, keeps the demons from being able to leech me. It confuses them for sure. They don't know what I am."

Hemingway chuckled. "I think most of us aren't sure exactly what you are."

"Ha-ha." Paris pushed the door to the apartment open. It was exactly as she remembered it with minimal furniture and lots of books. She pointed toward the back rooms. "There's my bedroom on the right and Uncle John's on the left. Take your pick."

"I'll probably sleep on the sofa." Hemingway glanced at the lumpy couch against the wall.

"Don't be silly. Make yourself at home. You'll be safe on Roya Lane. Just don't let any fae do any favors for you or you'll owe them a hundred years of servitude. Don't even ask them for directions. And don't gamble with the gnomes. You'll always lose. Oh, and stay away from the giants late at night. They're almost always drunk then."

"I think I'll stay inside and read." He indicated the bookshelves filled with dusty volumes.

"Well, you're going to need to eat at some point." She pointed at a coffee can sitting on top of the bookshelf. "There should be some money in there, enough to cover your meals anyway."

"That's okay, but thanks."

Paris lowered her chin and regarded him with hooded eyes. "Stop being so stubborn, would you? This is to keep you comfortable and oh, from being turned into a demon."

"I know. I just don't want to take your money. You're already doing enough for me."

"It's not money that anyone will be using," Paris argued. "And there's probably no food in the pantry."

"I don't feel right taking your money."

"Well, my family is loaded on both sides, my aunt lives in a mansion in Beverly Hills, and Uncle John only ever had us live simply because that's his style. Apparently, his electronic repair store is worth a fortune."

Hemingway chewed on his lip and nodded. "Okay, then. Fine. Thanks for all this. I'll find a way to repay you."

"Stay safe," Paris stated. "Not worrying about you is how you're repaying me."

He smiled softly at her. "Well, you're the one who needs to stay safe. You might be okay from the demons, but Agent Ruby is still out there, and he's dangerous."

Paris flashed a victorious smile. "Agent Ruby is going down, once and for all."

CHAPTER TWENTY-SEVEN

Paris hadn't been on Roya Lane for more than a few seconds when a black and white cat appeared next to her.

"I bet you scare a lot of people, randomly popping up out of the middle of nowhere," she said matter-of-factly, looking down at the magical lynx.

"It might surprise you to know that I don't randomly pop up next to most people," Plato replied. "But I do enjoy surprising Liv when she's picking her nose."

"How very charming of you."

"I like to think so." Plato strode beside Paris as she headed for Heals Pills, where she assumed she could find King Rudolf. Most didn't notice the cat, probably because he was using a selective disguising spell that allowed Paris to see him but not others.

"To what do I owe the pleasure of your visit?" she asked him. "Or did you happen to run into me by accident?"

"I never do anything by accident."

"Oh, then why are you here? Do you know how to find this fairy named Tiffer? Or do you have a way to get my father into fairy godmother places? I assume you already know what's going on because that's your style."

"I can't help you find Tiffer or get an invitation for Stefan," Plato said. "I am here to help you with something."

"Thanks. What's that?"

He gave her a sly look and didn't say a word.

"You're not going to tell me what you're helping me with, are you?" she asked.

"You catch on fairly quickly."

"Fine, you can surprise me." Paris pushed the door to Heals Pills open, grateful to see King Rudolf in the shop. Hopefully, this would be fast, and she could locate this Tiffer quickly.

CHAPTER TWENTY-EIGHT

"This is going to take forever," Ramy groaned as Paris and Plato made their way into the shop. She strode over to the counter where boxes surrounded King Rudolf and Ramy. Plato took a seat by the entrance.

"Oh, I knew I'd be getting a visit from you," King Rudolf said to her, smiling wide.

"You did?" Paris questioned, surprised. "So do you know why I'm here?"

"Yes, but unfortunately I can't help you," he replied somberly.

"You can't?" she muttered, disappointed immediately. "You don't know where Tiffer is then?"

"Tiffer?" Rudolf questioned. "That quack of a fairy? Oh, of course, I know where she is. I'm probably the only one who knows where to find her. I was saying that I can't help you with that other thing."

Relief flooded Paris' chest, but she was still confused. She looked sideways at the fae. "What other thing?"

"That one where we off Stefan," King Rudolf answered. "By now you've had an opportunity to get to know him and realize that he's the worst person in the world. I'm grateful that you didn't get any of his genes."

"I inherited his demon blood," Paris stated. "I'm fairly certain I got half his DNA."

"I don't think that's how it works," Rudolf argued. "My wife Serena is always saying that our girls, the Captains, got all her beauty and none of my brains."

Paris wanted to point out that he didn't have any brains so maybe they did get them from him, but she decided against it.

"Hey Boss," Ramy said, bouncing beside King Rudolf and waving a clipboard. "We need to get back to doing inventory, or we'll be here all night."

"How much more do I need to pay you to make this not my responsibility?" King Rudolf asked him.

"Oh no." Ramy shook his head. "I've had to do inventory for Heals Pills on my own for fifteen years because you couldn't visit Roya Lane."

"Because that would have compromised Paris' safety." King Rudolf indicated her.

Ramy stuck his hands on his hips. "Well, you're helping me this year."

"Yeah, fine." King Rudolf sighed, catching sight of Plato sitting quietly in the corner of the shop. "What's the lynx doing here?"

Paris glanced over her shoulder at Plato and shrugged. "I don't know. He says he's helping."

King Rudolf shook his head. "He rarely does. What do you want, troublemaker?"

"You have to get that cat out of here," Ramy said, backing up. "I'm deathly allergic to cat hair."

"You can't die," Paris argued.

"Easily," Ramy corrected, backing up more as Plato stretched to a standing position and strode in their direction.

"I need your help, Uncle Rudolf," Paris began. "You know where to find Tiffer? Can you tell me?"

King Rudolf shook his head. "Unfortunately, I can't."

She deflated, wondering how many obstacles would be in her path this time.

The fae stuck a victorious finger into the air. "I *can* show you."

"No, you don't!" Ramy complained. "You're staying here and helping me do inventory."

"We'll do it tomorrow," King Rudolf stated.

Ramy shook his head. "No, you've been saying that for months. It makes my job easier if we get it done. I'm not putting this off one minute longer."

"Is it possible that you can tell me where to find Tiffer?" Paris questioned. "Maybe give me detailed instructions?"

"I don't think so," King Rudolf answered. "For one, it's devilishly complicated, even for someone as brilliant as myself to figure out. Usually, it requires two people to play the game."

"Game?" Paris wondered if she heard him right.

He nodded. "Most don't know they're playing it, which is why you'll need my expertise. Also, even if you win and get off the train at the right place, that doesn't mean that Tiffer will help you. She's very selective about who she'll work with, but she adores me."

"Did you say train?" Paris asked. "If it's as easy as taking a train to see her, I can do that. Just tell me how to win the game and where to take the train to."

"I'm afraid it doesn't work that way," Rudolf imparted with pursed lips. "I don't know what the game will be like. No, the only way for you to get to Tiffer is if I accompany you. Maybe we can go tomorrow after the inventory is complete, and Ramy has sucked out my will to live."

"That sounds good," Ramy cheered.

Paris shook her head. "This can't wait. The fairy godmothers are in trouble. Demons are leeching them."

"That does sound serious," Rudolf stated, turning to Ramy. "What do you say? Can we do this tomorrow?"

"No!" Ramy exclaimed, throwing his hands into the air. "Fifteen years I've had to do this on my own. You keep telling me you'll help me, then you disappear. I want your help, and I want it now!"

Rudolf nodded, giving Paris a consoling expression. "Sorry, my sweet niece. Meeting Tiffer will have to wait."

Paris hung her head, wishing there was something she could do to convince Ramy to budge on this. However, he seemed adamant. With her eyes directed at the floor, she noticed that Plato had moved and was right next to Ramy's legs, which were bare since he was wearing cargo shorts. The lynx winked at her before sliding up against Ramy, rubbing his cat fur over his skin.

"Oh, that feels nice," Ramy said, smiling...then worry jumped to his face as he realized what the soft thing brushing against his leg was. He looked down with horror on his face. "No, kitty. No!"

Paris expected Ramy to start itching or sneezing, but instead, he shook all over and toppled over at once, landing on his back—the quickest allergic reaction she'd ever witnessed. Having done his job, Plato disappeared, leaving Paris and King Rudolf looking at the dead body before them.

Casually, Rudolf glanced back at Paris and smiled. "Well, since he'll be out for a while, what do you say we go and pay Tiffer a visit?"

Paris nodded, smiling triumphantly. She had no idea how Plato knew how and when to help, but she was grateful that he'd volunteered for the job.

CHAPTER TWENTY-NINE

"I thought we were supposed to be catching a train to find Tiffer," Paris remarked when they stood in front of the bakery display cases in the Crying Cat Bakery. "What are we doing here?"

"Well, as I said before," King Rudolf began. "Tiffer won't help just anyone. She likes me because I know how to find her, I'm pleasant to look at, I make her laugh, and I know to always bring her favorite pastry. Oh, and I saved her life."

"I'm sure she's most grateful for the last part," Paris replied.

He shrugged. "Maybe. It was only because I called off the hit I had placed on her."

"So you were having her killed and didn't?" Paris questioned. "I don't think that qualifies as saving her life."

"Remember when I called off that hit at the last moment?" King Rudolf asked, looking over the display case of pastries at Lee—the assassin baker.

"Do I?" Lee replied sarcastically. "I had to throw the bomb in the opposite direction at the last moment, where it hit a prickle of porcupines. I was picking quills out of my butt for ages."

"Ummm...I have so many questions right now," Paris said, confused.

"I make it a habit never to answer questions from someone as short as you," Lee said dryly. "You could be a large child or an under-developed fairy or a tall gnome. It's impossible to know."

"I'm twenty years old and in perfect health as a halfling, as far as I know," Paris remarked.

Lee shrugged. "Furthermore, I don't trust short people. They're invariably up to something, overcompensating for their stunted growth."

"Right," Paris said, drawing out the word. "I'll keep my curious questions to myself then."

"Do you have anything with Hennessy in it?" Rudolf asked, scanning the rows of buttery-looking pastries.

Lee turned and grabbed a bottle of cognac. "I have this. Will that work?'

King Rudolf's eyes lit up with delight. "Perfect! That's exactly what I was hoping for."

"I thought you said that Tiffer liked pastries," Paris reminded him.

"She does," the fae answered. "I like Hennessy. It helps me to think better."

"Oh, is that what's been missing before," Paris muttered dryly.

"We're going to face the ultimate test, and I need to be as sharp as an elfin-made sword." Rudolf grabbed the bottle from Lee, looking at it fondly.

"You might have to settle for Ru being as sharp as a soccer ball," Lee said over her shoulder to Paris. "That should still get you there."

"You mean for this game, we have to win to find Tiffer?" Paris asked King Rudolf.

"Yes, yes," he answered, sweeping his hand at the pastry counter. "We'll take one of everything."

"No, then I'll have to remake things, and that's work," Lee replied.

"Oh, fine then." Rudolf glanced at the rows. "Well, we'll take two dozen eclairs."

"I don't have any of those," Lee stated.

"They're right there." Paris pointed at a tray of eclairs.

"Again, short people really do destroy my cheerful nature," Lee muttered. "I have plans of sitting in my underwear and eating those eclairs later, so they aren't for sale."

"Then why display them for sale?" Paris questioned.

Lee glanced up at the ceiling. "Gods above, if you're trying to get me to kill this halfling shorty, then deliver the instrument to do it with."

"You can't kill Paris," Rudolf said, sounding offended. "She's Liv's child."

"Everyone is someone's child," Lee retorted.

"She's my niece."

"Technically, she's not," Lee stated, picking up a butcher knife that was sitting right beside her arm. Paris hadn't noticed until right then. The assassin baker smiled with sudden joy.

"She's a halfling," Rudolf said in a mad rush as Lee brandished the knife, giving Paris a sinister stare.

"That sounds like an anomaly," Lee replied. "Probably should keep that mistake out of the gene pool."

"She has demon blood," Rudolf said, taking a step in front of Paris protectively.

Lee gave him an impatient look. "Are you trying to make a case for me to kill her? You realize that demons are bad, right?"

"Can we grab a scone and get out of here?" Paris didn't at all feel threatened. "I have a slew of fairies to save so we can restore love. Not to mention a madman I need to apprehend who's stuck in the twentieth century and trying to destroy fairy godmothers."

Lee gave Paris a measured glare for a moment. Then she grabbed a paper bag, stuck a blueberry scone in it, and handed it across the counter to her. "I'll let you live this once. I can't stand people who can't live in the present century. Go take down that villain and make me proud."

CHAPTER THIRTY

Since the Crying Cat Bakery was one of the few places on Roya Lane where portal creation was allowed, it was the perfect location in the end to start the adventure—even if Paris had to endure insults from Lee. She figured that went with the territory.

King Rudolf and Paris stepped through the shimmering portal to a wide dirt trail surrounded by lush green trees. The air was thick with moisture as if it was about to rain at any moment and the smell of the forest was a stark contrast compared to the city odors of Roya Lane.

Ahead on the trail was an archway created by a bridge. Directly under it was a small platform. Paris looked around, wondering which way was the train station. It was so quiet in the forest that it felt like they were miles from civilization.

"Where are we?" Paris asked.

"In nature," Rudolf answered, quite seriously. "Don't touch anything."

"Why, are there poisonous plants here?"

"No, I don't think so. They're so nature-y. It's impossible to regulate the temperature in places like this. Without a moment's notice, water will fall from the sky."

"Do you mean rain?" Paris wondered if she should have brought something to drink too. Maybe King Rudolf would share his cognac with her.

"Yeah, I guess you can call it that," he replied. "Mother Nature really needs to fix things here, if you ask me."

"Again, where are we?" Paris asked.

"Scotland," he replied. "If the locals talk to you, nod and smile. I'm convinced they don't know what they're saying half the time, so how are we expected to."

"I don't think we'll run into anyone here." Paris looked around, only hearing the sounds of birds in the trees and the *whoosh* of wind.

"Oh, I don't know," Rudolf stated. "Someone else might be catching the afternoon train."

"Where do we catch this train?" Paris asked.

He pointed at the seemingly abandoned platform under the archway. "Right there. And we're right on time. The train might be here soon."

Paris glanced down. "There's no train track. And what do you mean, might?"

"The Mystery Train shows when it wants," King Rudolf answered. "We better get to the platform. I heard a bird of prey."

"Are they dangerous to us?" Paris wondered if a giant falcon was about to swoop down from the sky.

"No, they signal the Mystery Train arriving." He strode for the platform.

When they'd arrived, King Rudolf sighed, unscrewing the cap from the Hennessey and taking a long drink. Paris glanced both ways down the dirt trail, wondering if she'd wasted her time with this convoluted mission. Her heart hurt for the fairies at the college and FGA who were suffering from being leeched. All she wanted to do was help them as quickly as possible, but doing that hadn't been straightforward. Now she worried that King Rudolf was leading her astray.

"Oh, good, the train will be here in a few seconds." King Rudolf put the cap back on the cognac.

A large buzzard swooped down from the side of the bridge and flew through the archway, gliding down low to the trail and flying in the opposite direction. It was quite the mesmerizing sight, but Paris had no idea how that signaled the train.

She glanced back and forth, not seeing signs of this Mystery Train in either direction, which she could see for quite a ways. "Are you sure? I don't hear or see a train."

King Rudolf nodded. "Yeah, you wouldn't."

"Right." Paris drew out the word, thinking that either she was losing her mind, or more likely, the fae had.

However, a moment later, to her complete astonishment, a train appeared right in front of them out of nowhere. It was a real train—or appeared to be anyway. Steam issued up from the front of the locomotive. The brakes squeaked as though the train had stopped instead of appearing.

A door to the main cabin opened, inviting them in. King Rudolf held out his arm in a presenting fashion, smiling wide. "All aboard. It's time to take the Mystery Train. Then the games will begin."

Paris gulped, hesitancy in her every move as she climbed onto the train, wondering what this game would be and hoping it didn't get her killed—or make her kill King Rudolf.

CHAPTER THIRTY-ONE

When Paris entered the first cab of the train, the conductor wearing a boxy hat and a uniform greeted her. His black mustache rose when he smiled, transforming his face, making him instantly look younger.

"Welcome aboard the Mystery Train, Paris Beaufont, and King Rudolf Sweetwater." The man bowed.

"You know my name?" Paris pointed at herself.

"Well, of course," the train conductor stated. "I also know that you don't know mine. I'm Peter Peterson."

"Nice to meet you." Paris thought that was a strange name for someone. His parents must have thought it was funny. She looked around at the elegant train cab. It looked like they entered a time warp and were on a train going across the United States in the 1920s.

"Well, since everyone is aboard now, we'll get going," Peter stated. "I'll go and let our locomotive operator know. Please take your seat. The dining car will be open as soon as we're at full speed."

King Rudolf took a swig from his bottle, indicating a cozy booth. "Good, because I'll be dry in a bit."

Paris sat on one side of the leather booth beside a large window that showed the platform where they'd boarded. Rudolf took the seat opposite her. "So what's this game we're supposed to play and win to find Tiffer?"

King Rudolf took another long drink as the train pulled away. Leaning forward, Paris looked out the window, wondering what the scenery would show outside the train.

"It's hard to explain," the fae answered. "All I can tell you is to pay attention to everything."

Paris watched as the scenery quickly sped by them, showing a blur of green. It was forest and more forest as if they were cruising through the Scottish hillsides, although she figured that magic would be involved and they'd be going somewhere else.

"Okay, I'll pay attention." She looked out the window.

"Not out there." Rudolf stretched to a standing position. "What happens outside the train is irrelevant. You need to pay attention to what's happening inside the train."

Paris blinked at him, searching the empty train car. "What do you mean?"

He started for the door on the opposite side, waving at her. "Come on. Papa needs ice for the rest of his Hennessey. Let's go meet some folks."

"You mean there are other passengers on this train?" Paris stood and followed him to the door. "Are you sure?"

He nodded confidently. "I'm certain of it. They're part of the game."

CHAPTER THIRTY-TWO

To Paris' surprise, the dining car was buzzing with people. King Rudolf was correct, and there were other people aboard the Mystery Train.

Again, Paris felt that she'd stepped backward in time and was in the 1920s. A very distinguished woman was wearing an elegant silk blue gown with a feather boa collar and fringe on the cuffs. She pulled a long cigarette in a white holder from her mouth at the sight of King Rudolf and Paris and blinked at them as if surprised to see them too.

Gliding her hand over her black curls, the woman extended a hand to King Rudolf as he approached her table, many large rings adorning her fingers. "Well, who do I have the pleasure of making an acquaintance with?" she asked in a dignified voice.

The fae took her hand and kissed the back of it, leaning down low. "I'm none other than King Rudolf Sweetwater, and this is my traveling companion, Miss Paris Beaufont."

"A pleasure." The woman puffed on her long cigarette. "I'm Countess Jessabelle Fairweather. I'd ask you to join me, but I already have an engagement, which should be starting soon now that we're off."

"No worries. We have a table." Rudolf indicated a neighboring table that said, "Reserved for King Rudolf Sweetwater and Paris Beaufont."

"I see you do," the countess said with a pinched smile.

Without another word, King Rudolf sat at the table on the other side of the train car, against the window. Green forest still streaked by outside. Paris glanced around, noticing a waitress on the other end of the car, speaking to a distinguished man in a gray business suit with his black hair slicked back. They appeared to be having a heated conversation, although Paris couldn't hear what they were saying. It was mostly their body language that suggested they were having a disagreement.

Paris didn't hide her interest in the two, remembering what King Rudolf had said about paying attention to what happened inside the train versus outside it. However, a moment later, the gentleman spun and marched to the countess' table.

As though he might get lost in the narrow car, Countess Jessabelle Fairweather waved in his direction. "Over here, Thomas!"

He pursed his lips and nodded.

Leaning in Paris and Rudolf's direction, the countess said, "That's Thomas Cheetah. He's who I have a meeting with."

"I figured as much." Rudolf held up his bottle to the waitress on the far side of the car. "Can I get some ice, please?"

Catching sight of him, the waitress in a black dress and white apron nodded and disappeared into the next car.

Thomas Cheetah slid into the seat opposite of the countess, sighing slightly.

"What are you drinking, Tom?" She puffed on her cigarette. "I'm buying."

"Oh, Jessabelle, do you really have to play games?" He sounded tired.

"Can't I buy my friend a drink without you thinking I'm up to something?" she asked coyly.

"Are you up to something?" he fired back.

She batted her eyelashes at him in a flirtatious manner. "Oh, Tom, you know that painting will look better in my penthouse apartment. Admit it."

He sighed again, looking out the window. "I knew it. If you wanted the painting, you should have outbid me. That's how art auctions work."

Countess Fairweather blew out a ring of smoke. "You drove up that price past my comfort zone, and you know it."

"Well, may the richer buyer win," Thomas stated smugly. "That's how a free market works."

The waitress returned, carrying two crystal glasses with ice, laying them down in front of Paris and Rudolf, but her attention was squarely on the couple beside them.

"Brittany, my friend and I would like a bottle of your finest cabernet sauvignon," the countess said to the waitress.

"I'll take a whiskey neat," Thomas corrected.

"Oh, do you have to be so difficult?" the countess asked him, irritation heavy on her face.

"Yes," he stated at once.

"Fine, a dry martini for me," Jessabelle said to the waitress.

Brittany turned at once, marching back in the opposite direction, not taking a drink order from Paris or Rudolf.

"Interesting," the fae said to Paris, also watching the exchange and not hiding his eavesdropping.

"What are we supposed to be doing here?" Paris whispered.

He poured the rest of the bottle into the two glasses and slid one over to her. "Watching."

Paris nodded minutely, taking a sip of the Hennessey.

The countess and Thomas Cheetah appeared to be locked in a staring contest when the waitress returned with their drinks. She slid them onto the table in front of the couple and swung around to face Paris and Rudolf.

"Can I get you two anything else?" she asked them.

"Your name, for starters," King Rudolf stated, draining his drink.

"Brittany Jenkins," she stated, putting her hand on her hip.

"I'll take a bottle of cognac," he stated, looking at Paris. "And you?"

She shook her head. "I'm good. Thanks."

"Fine," Brittany said, as if not ordering something was offensive to her. She strode back the way she'd come, nearly running into a man wearing a pinstriped suit and a troubled expression. He had gray hair and a trimmed beard and appeared to be drunk, his glass of whiskey sloshing around as he strode in their direction. It also could have been the movement of the train though, Paris reasoned.

"Hey, good day, chap," the man boomed, setting his glass of whiskey down on the table beside Thomas and Jessabelle before taking a seat next to them. "I thought I'd find you two here, fighting as usual."

"We're not fighting," Jessabelle fired back, crossing her arms.

"Of course we are," Thomas argued. "It's what we do best."

"I swear, you'd think you two were married, the way you act," the man stated.

"You know I'd never marry," Thomas stated. "A man like me doesn't tie himself to a train track like that."

An audible gasp fell from Brittany's mouth as she dropped a tray on the other side of the train car. Paris looked up, watching as the waitress stooped and picked up the glasses she'd broken.

"It's a bumpy ride today, isn't it, Brit?" the man asked.

She didn't look up but instead rushed out of the car at once, probably embarrassed by her accident.

Rudolf leaned across the aisle dividing them from the other table and held out a hand. "Hello, I'm King Rudolf Sweetwater. And you'd be?" he asked the gentleman.

He offered him a hand, looking as if he might fall out of the seat. "Oh, nice to meet a king. I'm Ronald Whittaker. Yes, I mean, *the* Ronald Whittaker."

The countess sighed and put out her cigarette. "Oh, do you always have to say that when you introduce yourself?"

Ronald waved, fanning away the smoke, nearly knocking over his drink. "Do you always have to blow that smoke on me like that?"

"Which one of these is mine?" Thomas indicated the two side-by-side whiskey glasses.

"How am I supposed to know?" Ronald asked. "Have them both. I'm going to get a nap. Then we'll review those financials, Thomas, old chap."

He stood at once and lumbered in the opposite direction, not paying attention to anything but his path.

The countess and Thomas went back to staring at each other, hostility obvious in their gazes. They didn't look up when Peter Peterson entered from the other side of the train car, smiling with delight.

He halted beside the table and withdrew a cigar from his breast pocket. "Mr. Cheetah, I picked up something recently, thinking of you."

"Is that a Cuban cigar?" Thomas asked, an eager expression on his face.

"Indeed it is," Peter stated. "I know how much you enjoy a fine cigar and thought it might make your voyage more enjoyable."

"Why, thank you." Thomas took the cigar, running it under his nose, fondly. "That was very kind of you."

Brandishing a silver lighter, Peter created a flame, holding it out for Thomas. "Think nothing of it, Mr. Cheetah."

The other gentleman's eyes flicked up, an edge of stress in them as he puffed on the cigar, getting it lit. He blew out a puff of smoke and nodded at the train conductor, seeming to dismiss him. Without another word, Peter strode back the way he'd come.

"A nice man, he is," the countess said.

"Yeah, I guess." Thomas sipped from one of the two glasses of whiskey in front of him.

"Oh, you don't like anyone, do you," Jessabelle stated tersely.

"What's there to like?" Thomas puffed on his cigar and swirled the whiskey in his glass.

"Really, you're infuriating. I could strangle you," the countess said, standing at once and marching out of the car, not having taken a single drink of her martini.

Thomas laughed humorlessly, shaking his head. He looked about to take another drink when his eyes bulged, and the cigar fell from his hand. He then dropped the glass, making it clatter onto the table in front of him, and fell to the side, stiff as a board, toppling to the floor —dead.

King Rudolf clapped as if this had all been a show. "Now it begins."

"What begins?" Paris asked, her eyes wide with shock as she stared at the dead man before them, lying on the carpet of the train charging along.

"Our game," King Rudolf stated victoriously. "There's been a muuuurder! It's our job to solve it."

CHAPTER THIRTY-THREE

"Solve it?" Paris ran her gaze over the man stretched out beside them. "That's the game? To solve the murder? Does that mean that Thomas Cheetah isn't really dead?"

"Oh, he is, and it sounds like he deserved it and was loathed by many, which will make our jobs more difficult, by design," Rudolf stated. "To get off this train, we have to figure out who done it and exactly how and why. Only then will the Mystery Train stop. and we'll find Tiffer."

"What a strange game." Paris wasn't as repulsed by the sight of the dead body as she thought. "Is it always a murder mystery that has to be solved to find Tiffer?"

Rudolf nodded, leaning down to inspect the body.

Paris picked up a napkin from their table and used it to pick up the still smoking cigar, afraid that it was about to start a fire. She blotted out the ash on the carpet and put the cigar in a tray on Thomas and Jessabelle's dining table. "So when you said that you couldn't explain the game because it was complicated, you couldn't simply say, there will be a murder, and we have to solve it?"

Leaning his head to the side, the king of the fae studied Thomas.

"If I told you that, you would have been on edge. Most don't react well when they know someone is about to be murdered. I told you to pay attention, and I hope you did. They presented us with everything we need to solve this murder."

She studied the two glasses of whiskey on the table beside Jessabelle's untouched martini. "So much happened at once. It seems that everyone hated Thomas. I'm no coroner. How do we know what the cause of death is?"

"We don't." Rudolf stood. "There are forensic spells we can do, but they'll take time to lead us to the cause of death. Even then, we have to know who did it and, more importantly, why."

"What if we don't figure that out?" Paris watched the green scenery continue to streak by the train window outside.

"Then we won't get off the Mystery Train." Rudolf rhythmically flicked his hands. Paris guessed he was performing the forensic spell to find information on the cause of death. "One time, I spent the better part of a year on this train. That was my first time trying to locate Tiffer and pretty much the reason I put a hit on her."

Paris nodded, gulping down the tension in her throat. "I can kind of understand why you wanted to kill her now."

He chuckled. "I was alone then and didn't have your keen eyes to help. Oh, and I was sober, which we both know isn't when I think best."

"I hope it doesn't take us long to solve this murder." Paris looked around the dining car for any clues. "The fairies at FGA and the college are suffering, and I need to save them."

"You will," Rudolf stated with confidence as the train doors on either side of the car slid back. Having been alerted by the fae yelling, "There's been a murder!" the others had come running. From one end, Peter Peterson and Ronald Whittaker entered, halting in shock at the sight of the dead man on the floor. On the other side of the car, Brittany Jenkins and Countess Jessabelle Fairweather entered, also stopping at once. The waitress covered her mouth as a scream ripped from her lips.

Rudolf glanced at Paris. "While we wait for forensics to come back, the most important work of our detective case begins. It's our job to question these suspects." He looked back and forth between the two men and the two women on either side of the car—shock heavy on their faces. "One of these people here is our murderer, and it's our job to find out who it is and why they wanted Thomas Cheetah dead."

CHAPTER THIRTY-FOUR

"I didn't kill him." Countess Jessabelle Fairweather strode back and forth in the open train car, another long cigarette in a white holder in her shaking hand.

Not wanting to disturb the corpse and also not wanting to stare at a dead man's body, Paris and Rudolf had moved the interviews to a neighboring train car. This one was open with chairs against either side of the windows where the scenery hadn't changed outside still.

"That's exactly what the murderer would say." King Rudolf sat casually in one of the seats, his legs crossed as he watched the countess' frantic movements.

Paris sat beside him, taking in all the nonverbal cues from the first suspect they were questioning. They'd sequestered the others to the first car where they were sitting in silence when Paris and Rudolf had left them.

"I'm not a murderer," Countess Fairweather argued, offense heavy on her face as she continued to stomp back and forth, her black high heels leaving small impressions in the plush carpet as she walked.

"That's for us to decide." Rudolf picked up his fresh glass of cognac.

"How did you know the victim?" Paris asked.

"We were friends," Jessabelle answered at once, blowing out a plume of smoke.

"Friends?" Rudolf argued, arching a discerning eyebrow at the woman. "When we saw you in the train car, you and Thomas Cheetah were arguing, were you not?"

Halting, Jessabelle threw her hands up. "Well, yes, but…"

"I believe the last thing you said to Thomas was, 'I want to strangle you," Paris remarked, remembering the scene vividly.

"That's right." Rudolf nodded at her. "If that doesn't sound like a threat of murder, I don't know what does."

Countess Fairweather gawked at them, laughing. "Oh, come on. That's an expression. I didn't want Thomas dead. I wouldn't dirty my hands on that man's neck."

"So you're not upset that he's dead, then?" King Rudolf questioned. "Because if you're friends, well, I'd be sad if one of my friends died."

"Of course I'm upset," the countess argued. "I'm in shock, can't you see? Thomas was always trying to get under my skin. He was an infuriating man, but I didn't want him dead."

"What were you two arguing about right before he died?" Paris asked.

"Oh, that was nothing." The countess waved dismissively.

"We'll be the judge of that," Rudolf stated with confidence.

She sighed dramatically. "Thomas and I are both art collectors. I have an extensive collection, and I'm always on the hunt for a prized piece to add. Recently, Thomas and I were at an art auction, and he kept driving up the bid for a painting."

The countess's lips pinched together, and heat flared on her face. "He didn't want that piece. I know it. The painting was Rococo, and I know with certainty that Thomas didn't like that style of art. He outbid me to make me crazy."

"Why would he do that?" Paris questioned.

"That was what Thomas did," she answered. "He wasn't happy unless he was cheating someone or taking something that belonged to them. He was an awful man."

"Also not a way that I would describe a friend." Rudolf took a drink.

"Fine, we weren't friends," the countess admitted. "We competed for the best art. We ran in the same circles. We often found ourselves in the same places."

"So, as the old phrase goes, you kept your friends close and Thomas, your enemy closer," King Rudolf observed.

A disingenuous smile flicked to Jessabelle's mouth. "You know all too well as a king that powerful people can't afford not to keep an eye on their enemies. If I took my eye off Thomas, that's when he'd swoop in and steal the best art pieces."

"It sounds like he had, outbidding you at the auction," Paris suggested. "What were you trying to get Thomas to do when you were arguing?"

"Give me the painting, of course," she answered. "He didn't want it. I was willing to trade one of my statues for it. I know how Thomas loves his Roman statues, all clogging up his family's estate."

"If you wanted the painting so badly, why didn't you outbid Thomas?" Rudolf asked.

Hesitation flickered in the countess' large brown eyes. "The Fairweathers have fallen on hard times. Our empire isn't as wealthy as it once was and Thomas knew that."

"So you couldn't afford to outbid him, then," Rudolf guessed.

Jessabelle shook her head, her black curls falling over the side of her face, covering up the shame. "That stubborn man knew it, and he didn't want the painting. He didn't want me to have it."

"So you killed him for revenge!" Rudolf exclaimed victoriously.

She gasped, covering her mouth. "Of course I didn't. I would never resort to such things. Who you need to be questioning is Ronald Whittaker."

"Why?" Paris noticed the glint of mischief rise in Jessabelle's eyes.

"He was Thomas' business partner," she answered. "If anyone could have benefited from his death, it would be Ronald."

CHAPTER THIRTY-FIVE

"How did you know the victim?" Paris sat across the train car from Ronald Whittaker, the second suspect for them to question.

Unlike the countess, Ronald seemed much more at ease, lounging back in a chair, his tan loafer resting on his knee. "That old chap and I've been business partners for the last year."

"Business partners?" Rudolf questioned, standing and striding back and forth in the train car much as Jessabelle had done. However, his demeanor was scrutinizing as he worked out the clues.

"We'd started a company together," Ronald answered. "A real estate venture. We both had a fifty percent stake in the investment, and it was doing quite well thanks to my genius decision making."

King Rudolf glanced at Paris with a calculating expression. She thought she knew what he was thinking right then. However, he could as easily be deciding that he wanted a peanut butter sandwich. It was hard to tell with the fae.

"With Thomas dead, the company will now be one hundred percent yours?" Paris guessed.

Ronald nodded. "Naturally. That was the agreement we had set up."

"So you benefit from Thomas's death," King Rudolf accused, pointing at Ronald, who didn't appear flustered.

"Oh, I bet that's what Countess Fairweather said, didn't she?" he asked, annoyance on his face. "You can't believe a thing that woman says." He laughed rudely. "Fairweather is the perfect name for her because when she wants something, she'll be all nice to you. As soon as she gets what she wants, she'll cut your throat and not think twice about it."

What Ronald was saying didn't sound far off from the truth, Paris thought. Jessabelle had admitted to keeping her friends close and her enemies closer. It seemed that she was using Thomas.

"What motive would the countess have for killing Thomas?" Paris asked. "They didn't appear to like each other very much, but that seems to be common rivalry."

Another chuckle popped out of Ronald's mouth. He still seemed inebriated from earlier. "People kill others for a lot less than a common rivalry, but that's putting it mildly. The countess hated Thomas Cheetah. He was always outbidding her at art auctions, knowing that she couldn't pay the high prices he could. I mean, despite some of his faulty decisions, our company was starting to rake in the dough. However, Thomas' considerable family inheritance gave him a rather large spending budget for silly artwork."

Ronald shook his head. "I mean, really. Two seemingly reasonable people wasting their money on art. It's absurd."

"Do you think the countess murdered Thomas out of anger and tired of being humiliated at auctions and losing to him?" Rudolf speculated.

"No, chap, I don't," Ronald answered at once. "I think she murdered him for that frilly Rococo painting she was obsessed with."

"Yes, but Thomas won the bid at auction," Paris countered.

He narrowed his judgmental eyes at her. "Oh, have you never been to an art auction and don't know how it works?"

"Shockingly, I haven't spent much time hobnobbing with snobs at art auctions," Paris said dryly, not sure if she disliked Ronald or Jessabelle more.

"Yes, you don't seem the type." Ronald ran his snooty gaze over Paris, obvious disapproval in his expression. "If you were familiar with how art auctions work, you'd know that if something happens to the top bidder before they finalize the paperwork, the prized artwork goes to the runner up."

"So Countess Fairweather will now get the painting," Rudolf guessed, striding back and forth again, excitement in his voice.

"Exactly, chap," Ronald stated. "Thomas was poisoned. Who was sitting with him and had access to his drink?"

"We're not sure how he was murdered yet," Paris stated.

"You laid your drink down next to Thomas'." Rudolf halted, narrowing his eyes at the man before him. "You could have switched the drinks. They were both whiskeys."

Ronald laughed as if this was the most ridiculous thing he'd ever heard. "Thomas might make many questionable decisions, but he knew how to drink right. We both preferred whiskey as our drink of choice."

Paris tilted her head speculatively. "You didn't much care for Thomas, did you?"

"I think you'll find that no one liked the man," Ronald answered matter-of-factly. "Many referred to him as Thomas Cheater because he'd do whatever it took to win, profit or get the upper hand."

"Then why would you go into business with such a man?" Rudolf questioned.

"Simple," Ronald chirped. "Thomas was loaded. Our business required capital."

"And you didn't have enough money to fund it on your own," Paris guessed.

"So you switched your drink with Thomas', thereby poisoning him," Rudolf speculated, combing his hand over his chin. "Now, with him out of the picture, the company is all yours."

"I'd had a drink from that whiskey before I entered the train car," Ronald argued. "I had quite a bit to drink and left to take a nap."

"But you didn't take a nap," Paris observed. "Why is that?"

"Because I ran into Peter Peterson and he was trying to sell me on a new business venture," Ronald explained. "Now that's a man with a good head on his shoulders. He'd make good business choices, basing the decision on reason rather than greed. Alas, I had to turn the chap down."

"Why is that?" Rudolf questioned.

"Well, he doesn't have the capital," Ronald answered. "He has the ideas and the drive, but I'd be funding the whole thing. Poor guy works nonstop to make ends meet. When his parents passed, they didn't leave him a single dime. I mean, they gave him that awful name Peter Peterson, then they died and gave all their fortune to their younger son.

"According to Peter, his brother is a real ingrate, squandering the family fortune. Anyway, unfortunately, I had to turn Peter down. A real shame too. I'd like to work with him. Not a single time I haven't seen him smiling. He knows customer service, treating all of us with such kindness."

Paris nodded, having remembered seeing Peter Peterson present the Cuban cigar to Thomas, knowing he enjoyed such things.

"You didn't much like Thomas as your business partner, did you?" she asked, having picked up on several cues that suggested this.

"Is it that obvious?" Ronald laughed. "He was always making illogical decisions. If he didn't have deep pockets, I would have never gone into business with him. I planned to buy him out once things took off."

"Or kill him and take the company," Rudolf accused, picking up his tumbler and taking a drink.

Ronald gritted his teeth. "I didn't kill Thomas."

"You did want the company all to yourself, didn't you?" Rudolf questioned, and Paris quietly had to commend his style of questioning.

"Of course. But murder? Come on now," Ronald argued. "I know it appears I have a motive to kill him, but I wouldn't risk something like that for money. You know who would, though? Someone motivated by love or rather a scorned heart."

"Someone was in love with Thomas?" Rudolf questioned.

Paris' eyes widened with a sudden realization. "Brittany Jenkins, the waitress. She and Thomas were together?"

Ronald laugh. "She wished. No, he was using her, but the broad fell for his act. Now, if someone wanted to kill him, it would be the woman who he dumped."

CHAPTER THIRTY-SIX

Apparently too upset by seeing Thomas Cheetah's dead body, Brittany Jenkins needed time to compose herself before being questioned. After consoling her with a hug, Peter Peterson agreed to interview next—joining Paris and Rudolf in their interrogation train car.

"How long have you known the victim?" Rudolf asked the train conductor, having resumed his seat.

"Oh, for quite some time." Peter looked much more regretful about the death than the other two they'd questioned. "He was often on the train, going here or there for business meetings."

"So you knew him well, then?" Paris asked.

"I don't think anyone really knew the man who was Thomas Cheetah, to be honest." Peter shook his head. "He wasn't the type of person who showed people who he truly was."

"You knew he enjoyed Cuban cigars?" Rudolf questioned.

"I make it a habit to know what my customers enjoy," Peter said, a proud smile on his face.

As Ronald Whittaker had said, Peter seemed like a genuinely nice person.

"Did you see anything suspicious before Thomas' murder?" She thought the train conductor was in an ideal position to see the various behaviors of the suspects.

"I can't say that I did," he admitted. "Ronald had too much whiskey, but that's typical on these legs of the trip. He's a happy drunk, and rarely do I have any problems with him."

"You were with Ronald when the murder happened," Rudolf stated.

"I was," he answered.

"What were you discussing?" Paris tried to corroborate the various stories.

"Well, he'd mentioned the countess and Thomas were fighting again," he replied. "I knew the two would be at it for most of the trip. Jessabelle was only on the train to try and convince Thomas to let her have the painting she'd lost out to him at auction."

"Is that right?" Rudolf leaned back in his seat with a glint in his eyes.

"It's true," Peter Peterson answered. "Honestly, it was the only reason that Ronald was on the train today too. They both wanted something from Thomas, and getting time with him is never easy. He's a very busy man, always riding the rail between his estate and his various meetings."

"This estate, where is it?" Rudolf questioned.

"On the outskirts of London," Peter answered. "The train goes right by it on every route. Thomas had his very own private platform installed there so he could get between there and his meetings more easily."

"Quite the man of show, exerting his wealth like that," Rudolf stated. "You'd think he owned the train."

"He practically did," Peter stated. "Without his business, well, I'm afraid I'd be out of a job. We'd have to minimize our use of the train significantly. Most days, Thomas is our only customer, but he pays us handsomely to use the Mystery Train."

Paris offered him a sensitive look. "Now that Thomas is gone, what will happen to you? To the train?"

Peter sighed, looking off. "I'm afraid I'll have to look for another job. Now they'll cut my hours so drastically that it won't be enough to support me."

"I'm sorry," she offered thoughtfully.

"Did you and Ronald Whittaker discuss anything else before the murder?" Rudolf leaned forward.

Peter thought for a moment. "No, I believe that was it. He was going to take a nap and grab some financials for Thomas before dinner when we heard you exclaim that Thomas was dead. That's when we ran through the train to the dining car."

"Right." Rudolf drew out the word, giving Paris a pointed look. They were both curious about why Peter didn't disclose that he pitched a business idea to Ronald right before the murder. Or maybe it was the businessman who was lying about the train conductor wanting to go into business with him. Still, the questions were: who was lying and why?

"You said that Ronald was on the train to see Thomas as well, right?" Paris asked. "Why was that?"

"Oh, he wanted to buy him out of their business," Peter answered. "I don't think he could take dealing with Thomas one more day. They were constantly butting heads on the train about various business decisions. The whiskey made for volatile conversations between them. Although Ronald was usually a happy drunk, Thomas was known for getting quite belligerent."

"Interesting." Now it was Paris' turn to draw out the word. There was another inconsistency. Ronald had said he was waiting to buy Thomas out once the business had taken off—not that he was planning on negotiating it that day. Something wasn't right there.

"Were you aware that Thomas and Brittany Jenkins were in a relationship?" Rudolf asked the train conductor.

He nodded, looking suddenly more somber. "Yes, and that had been another source of conflict on the train. Brittany idolized Thomas, having fallen for his charm and money. She would always get distracted as we neared his estate, about to pick him up from his private station."

"Having the fancy estate on display from the train was a way to flash his wealth around," Paris observed.

"I think so too," Peter said. "But Thomas was done with Brittany, having lost interest in her. He'd told her that she was a simpleton and they never had a future."

"Ouch." Rudolf hissed as if burned.

Peter nodded. "It was rather heartless, but that's how Mr. Cheetah was, and Brittany knew that. She thought she could change him, but I think that was very shortsighted of her."

"You can't change the soulless," Rudolf offered.

"Brittany would have fixed the drinks that she served to Thomas and the countess, correct?" Paris asked.

"Well, yes," Peter answered. Then his eyes widened with alarm. "But it wasn't Brittany. She'd never harm Thomas. She'd never harm anyone. She might have been heartbroken, but she isn't a murderer."

"People do crazy things when they're hurt," Rudolf stated.

"Not Brittany," Peter argued. "She's the sweetest woman. So very loving and kind."

"Well, if she's ready, we'd like to question her now." Paris rose to her feet.

Peter stood too, heading for the door. "I'll go and fetch her, but please be sensitive with your questions. She's still very shaken, and I know that she's not the murderer."

CHAPTER THIRTY-SEVEN

As Peter had said, Brittany was still distraught when she entered the train car for questioning. Her face was puffy and red from crying, and she had a monogrammed handkerchief clutched in her hand, which she used to wipe her tears often.

"I'm sorry for your loss," Paris said, realizing that Brittany was probably the only one sad that Thomas Cheetah was dead.

The waitress opened her mouth to say something, but only a croak came out before she burst into more tears.

"Did you poison the victim?" Rudolf asked in a mad rush.

Paris spun to face her partner with an offended look. "Remember the request to be sensitive. Brittany is very upset."

"I'd be upset too if I'd killed someone," Rudolf spat. "I mean, so far, she has the best act."

Brittany blew her nose on the handkerchief, shaking her head. "It's not an act. I wouldn't harm Thomas. I'm devastated that this has happened to him."

"Are you more devastated that he's dead or that he dumped you?" Rudolf asked.

Paris wanted to slap the fae, but she reasoned that they were playing good cop, bad cop at this point.

"It's true that Thomas had broken things off with me," Brittany said through more tears, "but I have to admit that I saw it coming. I didn't think I ever had a future with him. He was a rich businessman, and I'm only a lowly waitress."

"Money doesn't matter," Paris urged. "Who someone is deep inside is what counts, and Thomas sounded like a real jerk—taking advantage of everyone."

"I know, but I wanted to believe that at his core, he was a good person," Brittany argued.

"You wanted to change him." Rudolf drained his drink and shook the glass. "Is it too much to ask that you get me a refill?"

"Yes," Paris answered at once. "We're conducting an investigation."

"Fine." Rudolf sighed. "You fixed the drinks that you served to the countess and Thomas before he died, correct?"

"Well, yes, but…was Thomas poisoned?" Brittany asked.

"We'll ask the questions," Rudolf fired back, appearing to be having fun with the questioning all of a sudden. Or maybe it was a crying woman who was bringing out a different side of him. He didn't appear as at ease as with the others they questioned.

"The bottle that I poured from was freshly opened. I broke the wax seal myself," Brittany explained. "Countess Jessabelle had given it to Thomas when she'd come on board."

"The bottle of whiskey was from her?" Paris asked, this getting her attention.

"She knew it was Thomas's favorite. It was a twenty-year-old whiskey, and she had given it to him when they boarded," Brittany answered. "He'd then handed it to me for the bar."

"The countess originally ordered a bottle of red wine for the two of them," Rudolf mused.

"I didn't understand that," Brittany stated. "Countess Fairweather never drinks wine, but maybe she was hoping that it would soften Thomas up. That's why she'd given him the whiskey, hoping he'd cave and give her the painting they were fighting about."

"She'd given him the whiskey, and instead of keeping it, he gave it to you for the bar." Paris tried to work out the details. "The glass of whiskey you poured for Ronald, was that from the same bottle?"

"Oh no." Brittany shook her head. "That was Thomas's whiskey, and I wasn't pouring that for anyone else. I poured Ronald's from a bottle that was already open."

"Interesting." Rudolf stroked his fingers over his chin.

"Peter says that you were often distracted when the train neared Thomas' house," Paris began. "Were you worried about how things would be when you weren't together, and he was on the train?"

"Well, of course." Brittany wiped her nose with the handkerchief. Paris noticed the initials were T.P. "But I didn't kill him. I was going to quit after today. I couldn't bear going by Thomas's estate every day or seeing him on the train. Now it won't matter. Without his business, we'll all be out of a job."

"That handkerchief." Paris pointed at the linen cloth Brittany was holding. "Whose initials are those?"

Brittany glanced at the embroidery as though she hadn't noticed it before and blinked in surprise. "Oh, I must still have Thomas's handkerchief. He gave it to me when he broke things off when he first got on the train today. I broke into tears, obviously upset, and he gave me this, telling me not to overreact and make a scene."

"I think the real mystery is how no one murdered Thomas Cheetah sooner," Rudolf remarked, shaking his head.

"Yes, Thomas Cheetah," Paris said, drawing out the names. "So his initials would have been T.C., not T.P., right?"

Brittany shook her head. "Cheetah wasn't his real name. Few knew that, but I discovered it when I'd seen the guest list one time. Peter had left it out, and only legal names are listed there."

"So what's Thomas's legal name?" Rudolf asked.

Brittany's eyes diverted. "I'm not sure I can say. No one knows. Peter doesn't know that I figured it out or that I saw the guest list by accident. I asked Thomas about it at one point, and he told me the truth."

"Someone on this train murdered a man," Paris urged. "If you can give us any information that can help, you need to explain what you know. Otherwise, it won't look good for you."

Brittany had trouble swallowing for a moment. "Well, I don't see what help it can be to your investigation. It's only some family secrets. You see, Thomas went by the surname Cheetah, but his real name was Peterson. No one except the two of them, Thomas and Peter, knew that they were estranged brothers."

CHAPTER THIRTY-EIGHT

"Things just got a lot more interesting," King Rudolf said as he and Paris reentered the murder scene.

Thomas Cheetah's body, or rather Thomas Peterson's, was still sprawled out where they'd left it. It was more than curious to Paris that Thomas and Peter were brothers and the train conductor hadn't mentioned it. However, when putting together all the clues, there were a lot of curious pieces of information.

No one seemed innocent of committing the murder. Strangely, everyone had a motive, a means, and something that tied them to the actual event.

King Rudolf held out his hand, and a moment later, a Sherlock Holmes-type pipe appeared in it. He held it up to his mouth and pretended to take a puff, one of his eyes squinting as she pictured the famous detective doing when contemplating an investigation.

"So let's review the facts," King Rudolf stated. "I spent a lot of extra time on this train before because I threw out solutions to the crime. I think to make our time more concise, we are smarter to think things through and come up with one murderer, the motive, and the means."

Paris nodded. "So if we throw out conjecture, we'll be penalized. That makes sense."

King Rudolf chewed on the end of his pipe. "Tiffer is an insufferable woman who knows her power is in great demand and makes those who want it work for it."

Paris leaned over the table where Thomas Cheetah and the countess had drinks. She picked up one of the glasses of whiskey and sniffed, then the other, not sure what she smelled for, but thinking that if one held poison, she might pick up on it.

"So Brittany Jenkins prepared all the drinks," Paris began. "Which means…"

"She would have the perfect opportunity to poison the one served to Thomas," King Rudolf stated.

"Or the poison could have come from the bottle of whiskey that Countess Jessabelle Fairweather gave to Thomas upon entering the train," Paris imparted, holding up a cautionary finger.

"True," the fae chirped. "The poison also could be in Ronald Whittaker's glass, and maybe he added it before entering the dining car."

"The forensics spell will be done soon, right?" Paris asked.

He nodded. "That only tells us how Thomas died, not why or by who. So we have to work out what we know and that hopefully was revealed in the interviews."

"Countess Jessabelle Fairweather had a reason to want Thomas dead," Paris stated.

"Oh, for sure," Rudolf affirmed. "With him out of the picture, she'd own the art auctions. She came on the train today specifically to meet with him."

"Ronald Whittaker also had a reason to get rid of Thomas," Paris argued.

"And he or Peter Peterson lied about their conversation during the murder," Rudolf agreed. "Ronald said that Peter proposed a business deal, but the train conductor didn't mention that. So what would be the reason to say that to us or omit it?"

"Well, and Ronald didn't tell us about how the two were talking about Thomas and the countess fighting," Paris remarked. "Why omit that?"

"Of course, Peter left out the bit about him and Thomas being brothers," Rudolf pointed out. "But if that was my brother, I don't think I'd want anyone to know either."

"Yes, and apparently Ronald knew that Peter had a brother, but it doesn't sound as if he'd connected it," Paris mused. "He also was caught lying because he told us that he was going to buy Thomas out at some point. Peter said he was on the train today to negotiate that with him."

"The scorned lover has the most reason for murder," Rudolf stated. "I mean, people do things for money, power, and love. But murder, well, that's almost always a crime of passion."

Paris and the fae king were quiet for a long moment, both of them lost in thought as they studied the murder scene. There was a lot of information to consider. Also, there were a few pieces of glaring information that kept rising to the surface in Paris' mind.

She thought she could work out what had happened, but it wasn't the logical progression of events based on the facts. It was taking a few leaps of faith, and Paris knew they needed something more concrete.

As if the universe was trying to help her out, something sparkled around the dead man's body.

King Rudolf rubbed his hands together excitedly. "Oh, the forensic spell is about to reveal how Thomas died. If it was poison, it will glow where it found evidence."

A second later, three places glowed bright orange.

Paris searched the scene, taking special note of the details. Then she looked up at King Rudolf. "I think I know who done it."

He nodded. "Yes, me too. Are you ready to go and convict our murderer?"

Paris grinned, looking at the passing green scenery outside the train, hoping they would soon get off it.

CHAPTER THIRTY-NINE

All the suspects and Paris and King Rudolf gathered in the train car where the interviews had taken place.

As before, Countess Jessabelle Fairweather was striding the length of the car, smoking her long cigarette in its white holder. Ronald Whittaker was lounging in one of the armchairs, looking over his nails as if he didn't have a care in the world. Peter Peterson was anxiously looking between the guests as though concerned about their wellbeing. Brittany Jenkins had busied herself serving a round of drinks to all those in the train car.

Paris took the cognac she was handed with a polite smile. "Thank you for gathering here for what we believe will be the reveal and resolution to this murder mystery. We know that it's been a very stressful evening for everyone."

"Stressful doesn't begin to describe it." Countess Jessabelle Fairweather took the martini that Brittany handed her and sipped it. "One of you is a murderer, and I'm stuck on a train with you."

"Well, you say that as if you're not the criminal at large." Ronald sipped his whiskey.

The countess clapped her hand to her chest. "Me? I'm not capable of such things."

"You very much are." King Rudolf stood, his hands clasped behind his back as he revolved on the room of suspects. "What's important to remember is that each one of you was capable of murdering Thomas Cheetah. Not only that, but you all had the means, the motive, and the opportunity. But only one of you committed the crime."

"Well, it wasn't me," Countess Jessabelle Fairweather said in a shrill voice. "I hated Thomas. I'll be the first to admit it, but I wasn't about to go to jail to take him down. He probably hoped I would. Then he'd get the last laugh."

"You did give him the bottle of whiskey though, as a faux gift." Paris narrowed her eyes at the woman.

"I was trying to endear him to me so he'd give me the painting," Jessabelle stated.

"An open bottle of whiskey," King Rudolf added, throwing a scrutinizing gaze at the countess.

"It wasn't open," she nearly exclaimed, pointing at Brittany. "Ask her. She'll tell you it was sealed."

"It was. I opened it myself." Brittany nodded furiously.

"It appeared to be unopened," King Rudolf corrected. "When my partner and I investigated the bar, we discovered that someone broke the seal on that bottle long ago."

"I didn't poison Thomas!" the countess exclaimed.

"No, you did what you thought was worse," Paris remarked. "You knew that Thomas was a snob when it came to fine whiskey, but he really couldn't tell the difference. So you brought him the bottle of twenty-year-old whiskey, making him think that you were giving him something of great value.

"However, you filled that old bottle with bad whiskey and worked hard to reseal the bottle or at least make it look resealed. A waitress who hardly ever opened an old bottle of whiskey such as that on a train wouldn't know the difference because Brittany thought that if a wax seal covered the cap, then it had to be unopened."

"I smelled the whiskey you gave Thomas," Rudolf continued. "What you had in the bottle was the cheap stuff. If you couldn't beat Thomas at his own game, you were going to give him bad whiskey, hopefully a headache the next day, and humiliate him by telling everyone he drank bad liquor and couldn't tell the difference."

"Maybe that's all true." The countess thrust her nose up haughtily. "But I didn't kill Thomas."

"It's all true," Paris said with confidence. "And no, you didn't."

"Are you certain?" Ronald Whittaker asked. "My money was definitely on the greedy countess."

"Speaking of greed," King Rudolf said in a booming voice. "You, Ronald, had boarded the train with the intent of getting Thomas drunk, hoping to convince him to sell his shares of the company to you."

"I did not," Ronald argued. "I told you that I was waiting until the company was doing better."

"A smart businessman such as yourself would know that Thomas would never sell once the company was doing well," Paris stated. "No, the best time to sell would be when things looked bleak, and it would be most advantageous to Thomas to get out. So you decided that you'd get him drunk by leaving behind your glass of whiskey, knowing that he couldn't leave a good drink to go to waste."

"Well, that hardly proves anything," Ronald retorted, then sipped his drink and shook his head.

"You're right," Rudolf stated. "Which was why we searched your room for the financials you said you'd be reviewing with Thomas over dinner."

"How dare you," Ronald seethed in an offended tone.

"We dared," Rudolf snapped. "What we found was quite interesting. The financials appeared to be doctored, telling a tale of a company not doing so well. A smart businessman such as Thomas Cheetah, under the influence of whiskey, would have taken one look at those and decided to bail out of the company."

"Well, the company wasn't doing very well," Ronald stated.

Paris held up a finger, pausing him. "You told us that despite Thomas' bad decision-making, the company was. Your story isn't adding up, Mr. Whittaker."

"I did want the company," Ronald boomed. "Thomas was going to run it into the ground. What did he care if it did well? He had his family money. So what, that I was willing to lie and cheat to get my share of the company? I deserved it. But I didn't kill him."

"You did lie and cheat," Rudolf said victoriously. "But you're correct. You're not the murderer."

Paris and Rudolf both turned their scrutinizing gaze on the waitress and train conductor in the corner. They had both gone silent and white, not making a single noise.

"I didn't want him to die," Brittany wailed, nearly breaking into tears again.

"No, you didn't," Paris consoled. "You loved Thomas very much. You wanted him to marry you, but when he refused, you lost it, storming off and making quite the emotional scene."

"I was upset," Brittany explained. "How else was I supposed to react? He'd broken my heart."

"So you killed him," Ronald accused.

"Of course not!" Tears streamed down Brittany's face.

"No, it wasn't Thomas you wanted dead," King Rudolf stated. "You told yourself that he'd love you. That if he could see you for who you are, that you'd be enough. You thought someone else was the problem —flaunting her fancy ways in front of Thomas."

"No, no, no!" Brittany said in a rush, shaking her head frantically.

"What?" Peter stepped forward, looking between the detectives and the waitress. "What is going on?"

"Brittany didn't try to kill Thomas," Paris explained. "She did love him. Because of that, she believed the reason he'd broken things off with her was because of Countess Jessabelle Fairweather." She pointed in the other woman's direction, making her eyes pop open with alarm.

The countess pressed her hand to her chest. "Me? And Thomas? Oh, how absurd. I couldn't stand that man."

"No, you couldn't," Paris continued. "But what Brittany witnessed as your disdain for each other, she interpreted as lust."

Jessabelle laughed loudly, a ring of smoke popping out of her mouth. "That's so irrational."

"It might be, but it still was enough for murder," King Rudolf stated.

"I didn't murder Thomas!" Brittany yelled.

"No, you didn't," King Rudolf continued, looking the waitress over. "But you did try to murder the countess, didn't you?"

Brittany's bottom lip quivered. Her hands knit together. She looked close to bursting. Then she nodded. "Yes, yes I did."

"What?" Countess Jessabelle Fairweather nearly yelled. "You witch!"

"I thought you were the reason Thomas dumped me." Fresh tears rolled down Brittany's cheeks.

"He dumped you because you're a poor waitress and he was a bitter old man," the countess fired.

"You won't speak to her that way!" Peter cut in.

King Rudolf stepped between the feud, holding up a hand to pause them. "Now, thankfully for the countess, she was so consumed with making Thomas look like an idiot by drinking bad whiskey that she didn't take a single sip of her martini. If she had, it would also be her murder that we were solving because Brittany poisoned it."

"You tried to murder me!" the countess yelled, looking close to jumping across the train car and strangling Brittany Jenkins.

However, Paris also stepped forward, serving as a barrier to the brewing fight. "She didn't, and that's not the murder we're solving. Only one man died today, and we know exactly who did it, how, and why."

In unison, Paris and King Rudolf turned to face Peter Peterson, disappointed expressions of conviction on their faces.

CHAPTER FORTY

"Me?" Peter Peterson pressed a hand to his chest. "I rather liked Thomas. I think I was the only one who liked him for who he was."

"That's because you were the only one who *knew* who he really was, but even then, you couldn't let go of past grievances." King Rudolf started to pace, his hands still behind his back. "You see, Thomas was your best customer and treated you very well, giving you lots of business."

"Then why would I want to kill him?" Peter argued, throwing his hands up.

"Because as Thomas did all things to minimize people, the best way to humiliate you would be to make you depend on him for business," Paris continued. "So he created the private train station outside his house, making it appear that he was going to be the Mystery Train's bread and butter. However, he conducted most of his business in London according to the financial records we found in Ronald's room, which was close to his estate."

"There was no reason for Thomas to take the Mystery Train on a regular basis," King Rudolf added.

"He took it for meetings," Peter stated.

"He took it so he could flaunt his business and wealth in your face," Paris boldly corrected. "He did it so you had to pass his estate every single day and see exactly what you didn't have."

"What is she talking about?" Ronald Whittaker scratched under his beard.

"Peter Peterson is the older of two sons," King Rudolf began.

"I know that," Ronald cut in. "Peter told me that his younger brother was insufferable and that their parents gave him the family fortune. That's why he asked if I'd go into business with him." Ronald gave the train conductor an apologetic look. "I'm sorry old chap. It's not for me."

"Peter did make that proposal right before Thomas' murder because he knew that he was going to need a new job," Paris continued. "Because he knew that his very best customer was about to die."

"You knew!" Brittany spun to face Peter.

He lowered his chin, his eyes searching the carpet as if that's where he could find answers to this mystery. "No, I didn't know. I wanted a better opportunity. A new life. A way to take care of myself."

"You knew that Thomas was about to be murdered," King Rudolf countered. "Because you're the one who gave him the poisoned cigar."

Gasps echoed all around the train car.

"It was the cigar?" the countess asked in shock.

Paris nodded. "Forensics showed poison in three places at the murder scene." She held up a finger. "The first was the martini glass, which we all know that Brittany put the poison into the countess's drink."

Jessabelle glared at the waitress, looking ready to murder her.

"There were also remnants of poison on Thomas' mouth," Paris continued. "They were a direct match to the cigar which he'd been smoking moments prior and received as a gift from you, Peter Peterson."

"Why would I want to murder my best customer?" Peter yelled, his voice irate and his face flushed red.

"Because he wasn't only your best customer," King Rudolf said triumphantly. "Thomas Cheetah was many things to you, but the least important was a client. He was the guy who'd stolen the girl you were in love with."

Brittany gasped, covering her mouth, looking between Rudolf and Peter.

"He was your estranged brother," Paris went on, earning more shocked sounds from those in the train car.

"And he was the man your parents gave their entire fortune to, having always favored him," King Rudolf concluded.

"Thomas Cheetah, also known as Thomas Peterson, was the brother who didn't win gracefully," Paris explained to the captive audience of wide-eyed people in the train car. "He stole his parent's favor, convinced them to give him their fortune, and flaunted it in Peter's face every single day."

"Peter knew that showing his animosity was what his younger brother wanted," King Rudolf stated. "So he refused and served with a smile. But soon, he couldn't take it anymore. Thomas had everything that Peter wanted. So the older brother decided that he'd steal Thomas' business partner, create a rift with Brittany to break them up, pin the murder on the countess who had every motive and means to kill Thomas, then committed the crime. Unfortunately, Peter Peterson, all the evidence pointed to you."

Paris gave the train conductor a long look full of shame and remorse. "You, Peter Peterson, are the one who murdered Thomas Cheetah."

As she finished her conclusion, the brakes of the Mystery Train screeched, and for the first time since they boarded, it came to a grinding halt, bringing them to their destination.

CHAPTER FORTY-ONE

The scenery outside of the train hadn't changed much. It was still green for as far as Paris could see, but the forest had disappeared, replaced by rolling green hills. She stepped outside and welcomed the fresh air after being on the stuffy train. She drew in a breath, her eyes adjusting to the light.

"What will happen to Peter Peterson?" she asked Rudolf, who had snagged another bottle of Hennessey from the bar on the train and was wasting no time in cracking it open.

He took a drink. "He'll continue to ride the Mystery Train, playing a different part when the next visitor boards."

"Are they actors?" Paris was thoroughly confused and also impressed by the magic of the Mystery Train.

King Rudolf shrugged. "They're Tiffer's guards because she's a weird and wonderful woman."

"The train delivered us to her location, right? Where is this fairy?" Paris asked.

The pair strode alongside the train, which puffed steam toward the blue sky. It idled beside a small station as though waiting to pick up more passengers. However, a moment later, it disappeared as quickly as it had appeared in Scotland. With it gone, it revealed the view on the other side.

"Whoa," Paris murmured, looking at one of the most beautiful sights she'd had the pleasure of seeing in a long time. There were more sloping green hills, but the scene that stole her breath was the majestic castle on the other side of a glistening lake.

"That's where we'll find Tiffer." Rudolf pointed at the castle that rose in the distance. It looked like a fairytale backdrop with an arched bridge in front and the many turrets rising high above it.

"She lives in a castle." Paris was still in awe of the scenery, expecting a Pegasus to glide through the air in front of them or something else fantastical to appear, adding to the sight before them.

"Yeah, and she better be home too, or I'm going to put another hit on her." Rudolf took another drink.

"After seeing all the poisoned stuff on the Mystery Train, you're not concerned about drinking that?" Paris asked.

He shook his head. "Most worry about being murdered if I'm not drinking."

"Well, don't put a hit on Tiffer or murder her until I get an invitation for my dad."

"Here's a thought," Rudolf began as they made their way toward the castle, taking an idyllic winding path through the hills. "How about I put a hit on your father. Then he won't need an invitation to FGA because he'll be dead."

Paris rolled her eyes. "I was just reunited with my dad. I really want him to stay alive. Without the invitation, he can't hunt down the demons. So no."

Rudolf shrugged. "It was worth a try. I'd offer to take care of your demon problem, but I can't be around those smelly monsters."

"Because of their odor," Paris guessed, having heard that demons had the worst smell.

"That," Rudolf answered. "But also because they make the worst appearance decisions. I mean, really, horns and facial piercings and red skin. I mean, they make one bad decision after another."

Paris shook her head, disbelieving that she was having this conversation and realizing that she shouldn't be so surprised. This was King

Rudolf Sweetwater. She had fun being a detective alongside him on the Mystery Train.

He might be an airhead and a drunk, but he was also a good friend and pretty brilliant when he wanted to be.

"Did you bring gold to pay the troll so we can cross the bridge to the castle?" King Rudolf asked.

Paris paused. "What? Now we need gold? To cross the bridge? Why didn't you tell me that?"

He sighed. "I assumed you knew there would be a troll to pay. This is Wales, after all."

"I didn't know we were going to Wales. I didn't know that's where we are. Or that there would be a troll." Paris suddenly wanted to punch the fae. So quickly things shifted.

He nodded. "Fine, but in the future, when you take a mystery train from Scotland to find a nutty fairy, go ahead and assume there will be a troll to pay. I'll cover you this time, but you'll owe me a pound of gold."

Paris nodded. "Put it on my tab."

CHAPTER FORTY-TWO

Paris didn't see any signs of a troll when they crossed the bridge. King Rudolf said that was because he'd tossed the gold he was carrying into the lake preemptively.

"If you can avoid a conversation with a troll, always do," he warned. "They aren't the smartest creatures and will leave you with a headache and wondering if they stole your brain cells as well as your money."

Paris wondered if the fae knew that he had a similar effect on people. She also wondered if there was a troll or if King Rudolf had simply sunk a bag of gold in a lake.

"Do you always travel with a bunch of gold?" Paris asked as they neared the entrance to the majestic castle.

"Of course," he answered. "It's a necessity for a journey such as this. I expect that you didn't bring binoculars, a slingshot, an umbrella, or a harp since you didn't think to bring gold either."

"You did?" Paris questioned, looking the fae over. He was wearing one of his usual silk tunics with a long embroidered jacket over it—all of the colors bright and the patterns intricate.

"Naturally," King Rudolf stated as they approached a large draw-bridge that was up. A wide moat divided them from the castle.

Paris paused, looking around. "How are we supposed to get across? You already paid the troll."

"That was so we could use his bridge," King Rudolf explained, indicating behind them to the bridge they'd crossed. "To get the drawbridge down, which is also the entrance to the castle, we have to do something else."

"Seriously, we solved a murder," Paris stated. "What else does this fairy want from us?"

Rudolf gave her a consoling look. "Again, you see now why I tried to kill Tiffer, right?"

Paris nodded. "How do we get the drawbridge down?"

"There's a switch," Rudolf answered.

"Where is it?" Paris questioned.

"Well, I don't quite know," he stated.

"But you've been here before."

He pursed his lips. "Do you think Tiffer is one to keep the switch in the same place for each visitor to find?"

"I'm guessing no," she answered. "Can we yell really loudly for this fairy to open up? I mean, we did catch the Mystery Train and solved the murder and paid the troll. I feel like we've done enough to find Tiffer."

"One would think," King Rudolf stated. "She knows that her services are in high demand and makes us pay for them. No, you can yell until you've woken up the sea monster in the moat and Tiffer still won't answer the door. We have to bring down the drawbridge."

Paris leaned over the side of the bridge, staring at the murky waters of the moat around the castle. "Sea monster. Got it. So that's why we don't want to risk jumping or using another means to cross then?"

"I tried that the first time," King Rudolf related. He pointed at the side of the castle where there was a patch of shore. "I pole-vaulted to the land over there, intending to scale the castle walls."

"It didn't go well, I guess."

"I still have the teeth marks on my bum," he replied.

"Okay, this switch," Paris began, searching the area around them. "Is it on the bridge somewhere?"

"It's on the castle," the fae answered.

Paris nodded. "Of course it is. First, how are we supposed to find that?"

From the inside pocket of his jacket, King Rudolf pulled out a compact set of binoculars. "It's going to be small if it's like the last time. The switch will blend into the castle walls."

Holding the binoculars up to his face, Rudolf searched the area in front of them, squinting around.

"So that's why you brought the binoculars." Paris was sort of impressed but wished the fae had given her a heads-up about all this.

"Oh, there's the switch." King Rudolf pointed at the pinnacle to the side of the drawbridge. "It's to the right of that tower. Do you see it?"

Paris narrowed her gaze in that direction and noticed a little red circle on the castle wall. "Yeah, I think I see it. It's tiny though."

"I wouldn't be able to see it without the binoculars," he replied. "I guess you can see it because of your demon powers. At least your father gave you something of use."

Paris laughed. "Yeah, I forget that I have enhanced senses, speed, and power due to the demon blood."

King Rudolf withdrew a slingshot from his jacket pocket and handed it to Paris. "I think you are naturally the choice to aim at the switch. I won't be able to see it without these binoculars."

"Again, that's why you brought the slingshot," she stated, somewhat impressed.

"Also in case I'm napping, and there's a noisy bird nearby," he replied.

Paris gawked at him. "I can't believe you'd hit a bird."

He returned her look of offense. "Of course I wouldn't. I'm no bird killer. I'd shoot in their direction, thereby making them quiet down so papa can nap."

Paris knelt and picked up a stone from the bridge and lodged it into the slingshot. "I don't have a lot of practice with using one of these, not having been a young boy who liked to aim at things."

"It's easy enough," King Rudolf explained. "Pull it back, and once you've lined it up on the switch, fire away."

Paris did as he instructed, but the stone made a high arc, missing its target. She leaned over and grabbed a few more rocks, thinking she'd adjust her aim more on the subsequent attempts. Thankfully she picked up the technique fairly quickly, and with each successive effort, Paris got a little closer. On her sixth try, Paris hit the switch, and to her surprise, a loud clanging from the bell tower on the far side of the castle rang out.

In front of them, the drawbridge creaked and slowly lowered.

"Nice job," King Rudolf commended, taking the slingshot from her and placing it and the binoculars back in his jacket pocket. He then pulled an umbrella from the same pocket.

Paris shot him a confused look—dumbfounded for a couple of reasons. "First off, are you Mary Poppins?"

He shook his head. "How much cognac did you have? Do you not remember that I'm Uncle Rudolf? Oh, you poor dear, can't handle your liquor."

"No, it's because you're pulling objects out of your jacket that shouldn't fit in there," she explained.

"You'd be surprised what I have in this jacket," he said proudly, opening the umbrella over them and stepping close to her.

"Second, why exactly do we need an umbrella, and why are you standing so close?" Paris asked.

A high-pitched wail drowned out any reply that King Rudolf could have made to her question. Paris tensed, looking at the side of the moat as a huge green sea serpent lunged out of the water. Thankfully it didn't try to attack them but instead jerked wildly back and forth in the water, slapping its body against the surface like an out-of-control large snake.

Dirty water from the moat sprayed into the air and rained down on them. However, thanks to the umbrella, Paris and Rudolf remained dry.

She smiled up at the fae, again impressed by his genius. "Wow, you thought of everything."

"I wish that were true," he replied. "If it were, I would have brought sushi. Seeing that eel-looking monster always gives me a craving for raw fish."

The drawbridge had lowered all the way, showing a grand entrance into the castle. Offering her his arm, King Rudolf said, "Are you ready to meet the most powerful fairy in the world who also happens to be the biggest pain in my ass?"

"When you put it that way, I don't know how I could resist."

CHAPTER FORTY-THREE

The interior of the castle was extraordinary. Paris had heard that castles were usually dank and dark places meant to protect queens and kings and not the luxury fortresses that many thought. However, Tiffer's castle was an exception and constructed with all the finer things in mind.

After striding across the drawbridge, King Rudolf and Paris entered an expansive courtyard filled with flowers and singing birds. Plants dripping with lush flowers filled the curtain walls surrounding them. Ivory covered the flanking and corner towers. Paris only got a hint of the fancy and regal furniture in the castle's interior that winked at them through the neighboring archways. She didn't expect that she'd get an opportunity to run her hands over the fine furniture since a woman was standing in the middle of the courtyard beside an elegant table that appeared set for a fine feast.

Paris assumed the woman with pink fairy wings and wearing the velvet robes was Tiffer. She better be or after all the hoops she had to jump through to get here, she was going to murder this person.

The woman gave King Rudolf a calm look when he broke away from Paris and strode in her direction.

"Well, Tiffer, you look quite well." Rudolf took her hand and kissed the back of it. "And like the complete pain in the ass that you are."

The fairy forced a smile. "You look like you've lost a few hundred new brain cells. How are your wife and the Captains?"

"They're my reason for breathing every single day." He released her hand. "As Serena says, my life makes hers possible."

"I don't think you understand what that phrase means." Tiffer glanced at Paris. "You've taken a mistress. I knew it was only a matter of time."

King Rudolf gasped, looking over his shoulder at Paris. "Really! That's my niece. Tiffer, it's only been a minute, and you've already offended me."

The fairy nodded. "It's a gift of mine." She looked Paris over with a discerning eye. Tiffer didn't appear young or old but was definitely beautiful. "You've gone to great lengths to see me."

Paris nodded, taking the position next to Rudolf. "Yes, we solved the murder, found the switch, hit it, and survived the sea monster."

"I meant dealing with this one." Tiffer indicated Rudolf.

"Two times you've offended me," Rudolf muttered.

"I will make it an easy dozen by the time you leave here in approximately two hours," Tiffer stated in a dignified manner.

"We can't stay that long," Paris cut in. "I'm in a hurry, and trying to get to you has taken longer than I expected. You see—"

"You need an invitation for your father to enter FGA, Matters of the Heart office, and Happily Ever After College," Tiffer interrupted.

"Well, yes," Paris answered. "Because—"

"He's a demon hunter for the House of Fourteen as a Warrior, and there seems to be an infestation at these three locations," Tiffer stated.

"If you know all that, why haven't you helped or made it easier for us to see you?" Paris was confused.

King Rudolf rolled his eyes. "Because she's a complete pain in the ass."

"Because it isn't my job to intervene in such matters," Tiffer corrected. "I've always been willing to help those who ask, though."

"Only if they derailed their entire life, riding the rails of the Mystery Train. Solved a murder and traveled to freaking Wales," Rudolf stated. "Then figured out the riddle that is your castle to gain entry."

Tiffer harrumphed. "I admit I only help those who know how to help themselves, finding me by using their mind. My assistance isn't cheap or handed out to just anyone."

"Well, we made it here, and since you know why we need your help, maybe we can cut to the chase," Paris offered, impatience seeping into her voice. Not only was she exhausted from all the adventures, but she was starving, not having eaten in...well, she'd forgotten how long.

"Although I'm a master of efficiency, there are certain things that do take time," Tiffer began. "For starters, your stomach is growling so loud that we won't be able to negotiate the terms of my conditions over that noise."

Paris' hands went for her stomach as it rumbled on cue. "Terms of your conditions?"

"Pain...in...the...ass." Rudolf paused after each word. "What did I tell you?"

"Although I'm happy to offer help," Tiffer began. "I really can't do it willy-nilly. If you need an invitation to those three places, it will come with stipulations."

"Oh, okay," Paris said. "Well, let's get to negotiating."

Tiffer turned to the table set with fine china, embroidered linens, and fresh flowers, holding out a presenting hand. A moment later, covered dishes and a tea service all appeared. "First, we dine. I believe Rudolf brought me a single blueberry scone because he's an unthoughtful jerk who knows I'm allergic to berries."

"You're welcome," he mumbled. "That was three times you've offended me. I forgot about the allergy and thought you loved them."

"Because you're a dimwit." Tiffer pulled out a seat.

"Four times," he chirped, also trotting over to a chair.

"Regardless, I have to take my tea so you all can join me." Tiffer waved at Paris. "Now, please pull up a seat and fill your stomach. Then we'll discuss what I require from you."

CHAPTER FORTY-FOUR

King Rudolf pulled the smashed blueberry scone from the inside pocket of his Mary Poppin's-like coat and held it up. "So you don't want this then?"

Tiffer shook her head, taking a seat. "No, I'd prefer for my face not to swell up to the size of a watermelon, but thank you, donkey's butt."

"Five times," the fae muttered, also taking a seat.

"You'll still help me even though I didn't bring something to trade with you?" Paris asked. "King Rudolf said the pastry was necessary."

"Making your niece call you by your title," Tiffer said to the fae with a disapproving look. "How very pompous of you."

"Six times," he chirped, starting to look amused by the insults at this point. "And no, I don't make Paris do anything."

"I call Rudolf all sorts of things," Paris remarked, thinking of her mother's name for him of Ru.

"I do too," Tiffer agreed. "None of them are appropriate to say at a dinner table though."

"Seven times," he sang, slathering a plain scone with clotted cream.

On a three-tiered stand were the most scrumptious-looking sandwiches Paris had ever seen. That was impressive since she was no stranger to seeing Chef Ash's food, and he always made things look delicious. She grabbed a couple of sandwiches and put one on her plate and the other in her mouth, hunger overwhelming her.

Tiffer picked up a teapot covered in floral print and poured for everyone. "No, Paris, I'll still help you even though you didn't bring me a gift, which is standard."

"I'm sorry," she replied through a mouthful. "My reason for seeing you is an emergency, and I've been going nonstop since this demon problem started."

"Understandable," Tiffer stated. "Now, the terms and agreement of me offering an invitation to Stefan Ludwig to three private fairy locations are quite simple."

Paris blinked at the fairy in disbelief. Nothing about getting to Tiffer had been simple or easy so she doubted the agreement would be.

Rudolf added cognac to his tea before sipping. "Yeah, you probably have to give this witch your firstborn or chop off a finger."

"Don't be ridiculous," Tiffer spat. "What use would I have for a finger?"

"Do I have to give you my firstborn then?" Paris sipped her tea and wished that Rudolf would share his cognac.

"You're a hybrid," Tiffer stated plainly.

"I'm not sure how that's relevant." Rudolf popped a grape into his mouth and chewed.

The fairy glanced at him with pure disdain. "Well, I realize that you have the brains of a marshmallow and therefore have forgotten that mules can't breed."

"Eight times." Rudolf drained his tea. "Again, I'm not sure how that's relevant."

"Paris is a mule," Tiffer stated.

To her surprise, Paris blinked in offended surprise. "I'm sorry, what?"

Tiffer offered a polite smile full of an apology. "Obviously, I don't mean that you're an actual mule. You're beautiful and quite the unique specimen, full of so much untapped and tapped potential. You'll go on to do many extraordinary things. Unfortunately, like a mule that is the offspring of a donkey and horse, you can't breed."

Something invisible hit Paris in the chest suddenly, knocking the air out of her.

"That's nine times," Rudolf said.

"I wasn't talking to you," Tiffer stated.

"I'm offended for my niece," Rudolf retorted, anger flickering to his face for the first time that Paris had ever witnessed on the fae. "How dare you tell her something like that so casually over afternoon tea."

"Well, I think it's better than me telling her on an empty stomach," Tiffer replied. She turned to Paris. "Would you like some sherry?"

Unable to swallow or respond suddenly, Paris nodded. She hadn't seen this coming, but it did make sense.

The fairy snapped her fingers, and a small glass and bottle of sherry appeared on the table beside her.

Rudolf reached over and poured Paris a glass, pushing it in her direction when he finished. "Don't listen to Tiffer. Serena and I weren't supposed to have children since she's a mortal and I'm a fae, but we did."

"Serena was also dead for the better part of a hundred years before King Rudolf married her," Tiffer explained casually, picking up a cream puff. "So you might not want to use him as an example of what's possible."

"You should," Rudolf urged to Paris. "I don't limit myself, and you shouldn't either. If you want to have children, then you will. I'll help you. Well...not like that. But I'll find an expert, or I'll become one. If my niece wants an offspring, she will have one."

Paris smiled, draining the glass of sherry. "Thanks. For now, I'd like to focus my energy on helping get rid of the demons plaguing the fairy godmothers."

"Right," Tiffer stated with enthusiasm. "And I was saying that I wasn't going to require your firstborn child as part of the terms and agreement to help because you won't be having one or any."

"That's ten times." Rudolf poured more cognac into his teacup.

Tiffer glanced at her watch. "Maybe you won't be here two hours then. Anyway, all I require is that you chaperone your father at all three locations, Paris."

She blinked at the fairy in confusion. "You mean I have to go with him when he hunts the demons at FGA, Matters of the Heart, and Happily Ever After College?"

"That's right," Tiffer affirmed.

"That doesn't seem like such a big deal," Paris countered, raising an eyebrow and wondering what the catch was.

"You've obviously never been around demons." Rudolf scrunched up his nose. "They smell like rotting flesh."

"That won't be the hardest part," Tiffer explained. "You see, demons don't go down without a fight or trying to flee. So there will be violence. There will be chaos. They will run."

Paris shrugged. "My father is fast. He'll run after them. His job is to kill demons."

"Then you better run after him," Tiffer stated. "While at these locations that I'll grant him and you access to, you must keep your father in sight at all times. If you don't, the binding spell I'll put on the portals will break, and your father will magically find himself somewhere else that isn't a fairy godmother location."

"Wait, what?" Paris asked. "I have to have my eyes on him at all times? Why?"

Tiffer took her time answering, chewing on the cream puff first. "You're a fairy in training to be a godmother. Even as such, you don't have portal access to FGA and definitely not Matters of the Heart."

"Well, there are unique circumstances," Paris argued. "There are demons there."

"I understand that," Tiffer countered. "Regardless of circumstances, I can't willy-nilly allow a magician with demon blood into two of the three holiest locations."

Paris watched as Rudolf poured her another glass of sherry before looking at the fairy. "My father is a demon hunter."

"As far as I'm concerned, he's a diabolical loose wire," Tiffer stated.

Rudolf threw up his hands. "We finally agree on something."

"I also say the same about you, King Rudolf," Tiffer said.

"That's eleven times," he muttered, finishing the bottle of cognac straight into his mouth.

Tiffer turned her attention to Paris. "Looks like we've almost finished here then. You look horrible, dear. When did you sleep last?"

"I can't remember," she answered honestly.

"Well, I require that you sleep before you go to chaperone your father at these locations," she stated. "Besides, your squirrel friend will be very cross with you for not taking him on this adventure after you promised to the last time."

"How do you know all this?" Paris asked.

"I gossip with house flies, Brownies, and spiders," Tiffer answered.

Rudolf nodded. "Yeah, that makes sense, you batty fairy."

"Unsurprisingly, most of the house flies say more intelligent things than you," Tiffer criticized.

Rudolf stood, staring down at the fairy. "I've had enough of your insults."

She nodded, looking quite pleased with herself. "Well, that was a dozen times, so that seems about right."

Tiffer snapped her fingers, and a cylindrical object appeared on the table beside Paris. It was the size of a screwdriver. The fairy pointed at it. "That's how you'll open the portals to the three locations. As I said, your father will only be allowed in there while you have your eyes on him. If you look away, he disappears into another room, or you even blink for too long, he will be tossed from his location and not allowed to return. You'll only get one chance."

Paris picked up the strange device. "This will open the portals? What is it?"

Tiffer winked. "It's magic."

CHAPTER FORTY-FIVE

"I can't believe you left me behind again." Faraday was cross with Paris when she returned from her adventure, as Tiffer had predicted.

"I couldn't find you, and I didn't have a chance to search the college," Paris argued, yawning as she crawled into bed. The fairy was also correct about her needing rest. She had messaged her father upon returning with the magic screwdriver, as she was calling it, that would open the portals for them.

"You went on the Mystery Train," Faraday complained from the dresser. "Do you know how much I love a good murder?"

"Saying that out loud is as weird as you'd think."

"Mystery," Faraday added. "You know how much I love a good murder mystery."

"Well, it was pretty fun," Paris stated. "I'm sure your deduction skills would have come in handy."

"Then you'll take me along for this mission to hunt down demons," Faraday stated.

Paris laid back in her bed, exhausted. "I guess, but I can't keep up with a squirrel running around. I have to keep a constant eye on my father."

"Well, then you need me," Faraday offered. "I can run errands for you or do things to ensure you always have him in your sights."

"How do you plan on doing that?" Paris asked.

"Science," Faraday answered at once, hopping into his sock drawer for the night. "As a bonus, I'll get to go to FGA and Matters of the Heart office. It's always nice to add new locations to my passport of magical places."

"You do realize that we're going to hunt down demons and not to vacation, right?" Paris tried to block out the visual of seeing all the lethargic students at Happily Ever After College when she returned. More than anything, she wanted to help the fairies by getting rid of the demons leeching them. But she knew that Tiffer was right, and she needed rest.

First, she'd sleep so that she didn't fall down on the job of watching her father while he hunted demons. Then, after they exterminated the infestation, she'd go after Agent Ruby—taking him down once and for all.

CHAPTER FORTY-SIX

Excitement welled up in Paris' insides at the thought of all that lay before her. It was surreal to think that she was about to go on a mission with her father. That layered over the fact that she had a father, and he was standing in front of her in the Fantastical Armory looking over various weapons. Even stranger was that standing beside her was Father Time, looking like a dirty hippy. If all that wasn't strange enough, Paris was still trying to wrap her brain around the fact that she was going on a demon-hunting expedition with her father and a talking squirrel.

"Do you have anything giant-made?" Stefan asked Subner as he leaned over the display case of knives, inspecting them for the right one.

The grumpy elf arched an eyebrow at Stefan from the other side of the glass counter. "The giants don't relinquish weapons very often. Why don't you borrow Liv's sword?"

"Because it's hers," the demon hunter replied. "Bellator hasn't and wouldn't bond to me. Since I've been gone, demons have gotten stronger after going unchecked. I'll need an arsenal of weapons to take these demons down."

"Not to mention they've been leeching fairies and are much more powerful for it," Papa Creola said. He had his stringy hair pulled back in a ponytail and was wearing a tie-dye t-shirt that read, "Knock on the door to my soul, and you will find an ageless hippie with a rock and roll heart."

Stefan nodded, combing his hand through his dark hair. Paris studied his piercing blue eyes and facial features, trying to decide how she took after him. She favored her mother a lot more, but she was half of her father—and got more than his demon blood from him.

To make it stranger, Stefan and Liv hadn't aged but a day when they were gone from Paris' world for fifteen years. So even though as magicians, they didn't age rapidly, they still seemed so much younger, and the gap between them and Paris only appeared to be ten or so years.

"Do I need a weapon?" Paris peered down into the glass case.

"Since you don't know how to use one and will undoubtedly hurt yourself, I'd say no," Subner grumbled, then added, "On second thought, maybe you should use a sword. I'll give you my sharpest."

"I know how to use my fists." Paris narrowed her eyes at the bitter man. "Do you want me to show you?"

Stefan snickered at their banter, used to it after watching the same thing happen between Subner and Liv. "I'd prefer for you not to fight any demons. I don't like the idea of you having to be there at all, Pare. But I'll keep you safe, and I'd recommend relying on defensive spells to protect yourself rather than offensive ones to attack. Leave the demon-slaying to me."

"Is this a real refraction lens?" Faraday asked from the other side of the shop. The squirrel was sitting on a counter and peering down at one of the artifacts inside with awe.

"It's not just any refraction lens," Papa Creola began, trotting over to the case. "Not only does it have prism effects, but it shoots, bends, and directs light and creates mirrored surfaces."

"What are they talking about?" Stefan whispered to Paris.

She shook her head. "I rarely understand what the squirrel is talking about."

"Whoa," Faraday said, his brown eyes wide with sudden excitement. "I'd heard a rumor that these existed, but I didn't think they did. They were supposedly full of so much strange magic, giving them all sorts of nifty uses."

The talking squirrel had nearly passed out when Paris told him they were stopping by the Fantastical Armory before the mission. The fact that he got to meet Father Time and see many of the strange artifacts in the shop made Faraday squeal so loudly that it hurt Paris' ears.

"This is the only one." Papa Creola reached into the case and withdrew something that looked like a small round monocle. He held it out to Faraday.

The squirrel's mouth was hanging open when he took the small device with both paws. "I can't believe I'm getting to see this in person...well, squirrel form."

"Well, you need to because it's now yours," Papa Creola said proudly, looking down at the rodent.

Paris thought Faraday might pass out. He went rigid all over, his mouth dropping open more. His paws shook on the refraction lens. "Are you serious? Me? Why?"

"Because you're going to need it." Papa Creola's usual air of mystery covered his words and expression.

"Me? I'll need it?" Faraday's gaze fell to the glass counter under him, his mind suddenly racing. "There are so many ways to use this. It's for the upcoming mission?"

Papa Creola didn't answer this. Instead, he strode back the way he'd come. "You know how to use it. Be careful and don't let it get broken."

Faraday looked at Paris with complete shock. "I got a refraction lens. THE refraction lens."

"What does that mean?" she asked.

"That I can die happy." He swayed as if he might fall over dead right there.

"Let's focus on you surviving." Stefan pointed at two long swords on the far wall. "I'll take those and a set of the giant-made knives you have over there." He nodded at a chest with a clear lid behind Subner.

"I told you that I didn't have any giant-made weapons," the elf with greasy black hair muttered with a sullen expression.

"You must have forgotten about those." Stefan laughed. "A giant clearly made them."

"They're the only giant-crafted weapons I currently have," Subner replied, annoyance heavy on his face. "I don't want anything happening to them."

Stefan flashed him a convincing smile. "I'll bring them back."

"You won't though." Subner turned and pulled the long swords from the wall.

"Oh, so you see how this goes down then." Stefan laughed again. Papa Creola's assistant, much like him, was privy to bits of the future. However, as Father Time had explained, revealing events wasn't advantageous for most to know and the future often changed. Nothing was guaranteed.

"I know that if I give you those giant-made knives, they won't come back," Subner stated.

"Can you tell me if I do?" Stefan asked morbidly.

The elf laid the swords on the glass countertop between them. "My weapons expert had a time trying to get those knives. I'm not ready to let them go until he brings me more from the giants."

"How about I get Rory to make you something?" Stefan offered, testing the balance of one of the swords before sheathing it across his back.

"He doesn't make weapons," Subner argued.

"He made Bellator for Liv," Papa Creola cut in.

"That was the last weapon he made," Subner grumbled.

Stefan picked up the other sword and also sheathed it across his back, the handles crossed and poking out at his shoulders. "If Liv asked him to make something, he would come out of retirement to do so. You know that."

Subner sighed. "Then she'll be even more intolerable, holding it over my head that she helped me out."

Stefan laughed. "Yeah, she would. But you bring it on yourself, egging her on constantly."

"She brings it on being irritatingly annoying," Subner spat.

"Come on, man," Stefan urged. "You know that giant-made blades are more effective at killing demons. I already have my work cut out for me hunting down three super powerful demons with my daughter having to keep a constant eye on me."

"With a squirrel in tow," Subner muttered, pointing at Faraday who was still marveling at his refraction lens.

"Exactly," Stefan chirped. "Help me out, would you?"

Subner sighed, turned, and retrieved the knives with thick handles and curved blades. "I want two knives to replace these and a sword."

Smiling victoriously, Stefan took the knives and nodded. "You got it. But don't discount that I might bring these back."

"You won't," Subner stated, "but I won't blame you for it." He glanced at Paris. "Like her mother, that one is the bane of my existence. She'll lose the knives."

CHAPTER FORTY-SEVEN

"What's that supposed to mean? How am I going to lose the knives?" Paris asked as Stefan, Faraday, and she exited the Fantastical Armory, striding to a place where she could create a portal with the magic screwdriver. Subner had trudged off to the back room after his conclusion, enjoying the idea of disappearing after that cliffhanger.

"I wouldn't worry about it." Stefan checked to ensure that he'd securely fastened his sheathed knives to the waist strap of his harness. "Subner was probably trying to make you paranoid. He loves any opportunity he can get to cause you or Liv stress. I don't plan on you using weapons or fighting at all, so I don't see how you could be the one who loses the knives."

"So I'm supposed to run around keeping an eye on you?" Paris wondered how this was going to work.

"Maybe we can find a surveillance room at FGA headquarters, and you can watch me from the safety of there," he muttered.

"It's not a bad idea," Faraday remarked, scurrying beside them on the cobbled lane.

Paris shook her head. "No, there's got to be blind spots on security cameras. We can't risk you being out of sight for even a moment. If you are, we've lost our opportunity for you to hunt down the demons. Then it will have to be me."

Stefan pursed his lips. "That's not happening. When you're keeping an eye on me, I want it to be from as far away as possible."

"I'm not sure if that will be possible," Paris replied. "The fairy that set the rules said that demons are fast, will fight, and probably flee."

Stefan nodded. "Unfortunately, that's all true. I can't predict what's going to happen. I want you to be safe, and I don't like this scenario at all."

"You said that my demon blood protects me, right?" Paris questioned.

"It protects you from being bitten, but not from getting hurt. When a demon is fighting to survive, it will maim or kill anything in its path. It's crucial that you stay out of the way as much as possible. I try to make their deaths fast, but I have to admit, these are mega demons I'm facing. They're strong and much more powerful than any others I've encountered. Try to be careful. If it's between you saving yourself or keeping an eye on me, save yourself."

Paris didn't respond to that because she wasn't going to lie to her father. If it came to her safety or taking out the demons, she was taking the hit. Her life wasn't worth more than hundreds of fairies. The demons had to go, no matter what.

CHAPTER FORTY-EIGHT

The streets of New York were busy outside the FGA headquarters when the three stepped through the portal. The lobby of the skyscraper in downtown Manhattan was empty, though.

Paris had expected the headquarters for the fairy godmother agency to be like the mansion at Happily Ever After College. She'd thought it would look and feel like a grandma's home with the warmth and ever-present smell of fresh-baked chocolate cookies. However, it was the complete opposite and instantly reminded her of the agents that supervised the fairy godmothers.

Much like the agents, the lobby was all sleek black, reminding Paris of the suits they all wore. The walls were all black marble, which didn't contrast against the black granite floors. Hanging overhead was a huge and modern black glass chandelier.

Her father shared Paris' surprise based on the look on his face. "I was expecting more red...or any red...or any color."

"Me too," she agreed, putting the magic screwdriver in her pocket as she studied the spacious lobby.

In contrast to the rich, warm wood all around the mansion at the college, the lobby of FGA was ultra-modern with straight lines and lots of sharp corners. The couches in front of the bank of elevators didn't look comfortable.

Many of the fairies had vacated the building, too drained from what the demons somewhere in the skyscraper were doing to them. Some had remained, too afraid of what could be lurking outside their previous haven, as Headmistress Starr had assumed. Willow had sent a message to the agents at the headquarters, telling them that a demon hunter would be entering the skyscraper. They had all moved to the middle floors since Stefan assumed the demons would be on the top and bottom of the fifty-story building.

"As I expected." Stefan sniffed the air and studied the lobby with a discerning eye. "There are two demons. One in the basement and I believe one at the top of FGA."

"The top story is the Matters of the Heart office." Paris had reviewed the building's floor plans before leaving the college.

He nodded. "Makes sense that they'd spread out so they didn't have to share."

"Going after Saint Valentine's office would be in line with Agent Ruby's mission to take him down," Faraday offered.

"Can you sense the demons?" Stefan asked Paris.

She tuned into her feelings, drawing in a breath. Inside, she felt conflicted, as if something was tugging her in different directions—fueling her with a strange desire.

"I want to go downstairs and up at the same time, so I think so," Paris stated.

"Do you feel compelled to stamp out whatever is there?" Stefan asked.

She nodded. "Yeah, it's as if I crave blood in a way."

"Embrace that," Stefan advised. "I know it seems strange, but evil repulses you, like me. You'll always want to rid the world of anything immoral. Although that desire can burn us out, it's also a gift. I've found that I'm much more objective if I embrace that craving rather than trying to resist it.

"Objectivity is key. If you have that, you'll know your limits. You'll know when the craving is controlling you, rather the other way around. If you lose control, you will kill yourself trying to erase evil."

Paris nodded, taking in her father's wisdom. "Embrace the desire. Stay objective. Stay in control."

"Good," Stefan affirmed, looking around the lobby.

"Do we go down or up first?" Faraday asked.

"Down," Paris answered before her father could.

He gave her a proud look, his eyes twinkling. "Why is that?"

It was a test, and he was trying to see if she knew the right answer. "Because," she began, drawing out the word and considering her reply. She answered right away based on instinct, but there was a valid reason. "The demon below is closer and drawing me toward it. Also, I don't feel that it's as powerful as the one above us. Taking that one out will give us an idea of what we're dealing with in these mega demons. Then we can better strategize how to take out the one above."

"Very good." Stefan smiled but pointed at himself. "However, I'm the one taking out the demons. You're my eyes. My supervisor. But yes, we're going down first."

"Great." Paris nodded. "Do we take the elevators?"

He shook his head. "Elevators, when in battle, are always death traps. Avoid them at all costs. The demons will know that I'm here, and they'll attack knowing that it's kill or be killed."

Faraday scurried off to a hallway. "According to the building schematics, the stairs are this way. Also, there's only one entrance into the basement, so we'll have the demon trapped."

"Good thinking bringing the squirrel," Stefan complimented and followed Faraday. Paris hurried to keep up and keep a constant eye on her father.

CHAPTER FORTY-NINE

The cold bit at Paris' insides as they descended to the basement. The slight chattering of her teeth caught her father's attention as he took the stairs beside her.

"Demons prefer extreme cold," he explained.

"That's surprising." Faraday's paws shook as he held the refraction lens.

"Yes, most expect that demons would like fire and extreme heat, but most prefer cold because they're so hot." Pausing at the end of the stairwell, Stefan studied a closed door at the dead-end of the hallway. He pressed his ear to the panel as though listening for the demon on the other side, but Paris thought he was using another sense to investigate—a sixth sense.

Glancing back at her, Stefan said, "The demon knows we're here. Remember that they're tricky and unfortunately pretty clever."

"And they smell really bad." Paris pinched her nose as the odor assaulted her. She suddenly wished she could turn off that sense.

Stefan nodded. "You never get used to it either. Remember to keep your distance from me. I have to get close to take a demon out, which is why I got bit before."

Paris drew in a breath through her mouth. Her father had said there were few ways to kill a demon. The most reliable was to behead them. The giant-made knives were helpful because a stab with one through the chest should be enough to take the monsters down. However, he was correct that those tactics involved getting close. Arrows were ineffective against demons. Guns, according to her parents, were for cowards and usually produced more problems in battle than they solved.

"What do you want me to do?" Faraday held the refraction lens although there was a small chain that secured it around his neck.

"Use your greatest asset," Stefan offered, pointing at his head. "Use your mind to help create advantages for us. Everything about fighting a demon is about strategy. Keep your eyes open, know that they move fast, and they don't fight fair."

Stefan yanked the door open, blasting the three of them with more cold.

CHAPTER FIFTY

Paris tensed at the sight before them. On the other side of the door was total blackness. She blinked, willing her eyes to adjust.

"Oh, one other thing about demons," her father said quietly, pulling one of the swords from its sheath on his back. "They loathe light."

Suddenly the light of the stairwell flickered, and Paris froze. They were about to be cast in total blackness. Then she wouldn't be able to see her father, and he'd get kicked out of FGA headquarters. And she'd be there…with a demon.

Stefan kicked the door back with his foot and withdrew his other sword, holding them at the ready. "Create a light orb," he ordered his daughter in a stern voice.

Not wasting a single second as the lights flickered overhead, Paris held out her palm and created a ball of light and not a moment too soon. The lights in the stairwell vanished, casting them in darkness.

The light orb resembled a ball of fire but wasn't hot to the touch. It reminded Paris of a crystal ball sending out rays of light that reached only five feet in all directions. She tried to magnify the spell, but she knew that would drain her magic reserves fast. Then they'd have zero light, and her father would disappear from her sight and the FGA headquarters.

It was as if she'd gone blind when Paris peered around, seeing only blackness in the area that the light orb didn't reach.

Stefan blew out an angry breath. "This is going to make it more complicated. On second thought, stay close."

Paris nodded, knowing that this did make things extremely dangerous. She had to be within five feet of her father to see him while he was fighting a demon and swinging sharp swords. The demon was clever, cutting the lights and making them shiver. It had the advantages.

"I think I can magnify the light using the refraction lens." Faraday held up the device around his neck as a guttural scream ripped through the air, echoing through the basement.

Stefan narrowed his eyes in the direction the scream came from, gripping his weapons in both hands. "Good. Make it quick. Things are about to get dangerous."

CHAPTER FIFTY-ONE

Paris didn't know what Faraday was planning on doing, but that was totally up to him at this point. She had to focus her energy on her father and the light orb as a demon burst out of the shadows, looking like the worst thing she'd ever seen.

Its skin was a bright shade of red, and small, curved horns covered its jaw and head. In the quick flash when the monster appeared, Paris saw several silver hoops piercing its face and black tribal tattoos on its arm.

The demon ran by in a flash, streaking past a foot in front of Stefan. He spun in the direction that it went, his sword slicing through the air, but the beast was already gone in a blur. The smell was assaulting. The noise the monster made, halfway between a growl and a scream, pierced Paris' ears.

She was so focused on her father that Paris barely caught the demon in her peripheral vision before it ran by again, this time between her and Stefan. Its claws brushed against her abdomen. Paris sucked in a breath as her father jerked to face her, brought up his sword, but stopped before whipping it down. He was too close to her — she would've been collateral damage if he tried to attack the demon and they both knew it, based on their expressions.

Again the demon was there and gone in an instant. The only sign that it was still close by was the evil cackle in the shadows…and the smell.

"It's toying with us." Stefan looked Paris over as if the demon might have cut her with its claws when it sprinted by. She guessed that it could have, but it was taunting them—trying to make her so afraid that she slipped up. Playing on Stefan's weakness to protect his daughter over all else.

Grabbing one of the giant-made knives on his belt, Stefan pulled it out by the hilt and flipped it around, handing it to Paris hilt-first. "Take this and use it if that thing gets close. Go for any part of it. The blade will do the work for you."

Paris nodded, realizing that her father had to change his mind about her fighting when they had to be so close at this point. With her free hand and thankfully her dominant one, Paris took the knife.

Again, the monster ripped by in a flash, this time on the other side of Stefan. He swung around so fast that he was also a blur, both swords sweeping through the air in an incredible display. The sound of a blade slicing through material and flesh filled the room, followed by another howling scream.

Black blood spilled to the concrete floor, but not enough and it trickled away as the demon retreated into the shadows.

Stefan had wounded the beast. That was something. But the fact that his swords had nearly brushed Paris again was a hazard, and they both knew it. The demon hunter let out a weighted breath as he glanced at Paris. He was too close to her to effectively attack the demon, especially with the game it was playing on them.

The light orb glowed brighter in Paris' hand, making her eyes flicker to it, still keeping her father in her sights, though. The light stretched out farther, and Paris' chest swelled with relief.

Aware of Faraday at her feet, Paris nodded in his direction. "Good work."

"I'll see if I can do even better," Faraday said, his voice calculated as he turned the refraction lens one way, then another.

The light stretched around them in all directions, taking up about a ten feet radius. That was much better than before, Paris thought with relief. With more visibility, she realized there wasn't much in the basement except concrete floors and open space.

Right when Paris thought they'd gotten their first break, freezing mist rose from the floor, covering their legs and making it hard to see what was around them, even in the glowing light.

CHAPTER FIFTY-TWO

The cold was somehow more assaulting than before. Faraday was instantly covered, and Paris worried for him. Keeping her eyes on her father, Paris knelt and held out her arm with the knife. With his teeth chattering, Faraday climbed onto her jacket to her shoulder.

She was going to have to release the light orb, letting it hover beside them since she was running out of ways to protect herself now with a squirrel hanging out on her shoulder.

The cold mist rising from the floor made Paris' feet feel frozen in place. It reminded her of when the Bewilder Forest froze when they'd exorcised Hemingway's mother. Even though the light orb floated between Paris and Stefan, casting light in all directions, the mist made it so she could only see his top half. It was thicker at the edge of the light, and she assumed that if he got too far away, she'd lose sight of him.

Things had gotten even more complicated, and based on his expression, Stefan knew it.

However, they had little time to strategize because after making it colder, the demon seemed renewed despite its injury. It streaked between them again. Paris slashed the knife at the monster but caught only air.

Not wasting a moment, the demon circled back, this time in front of Stefan. In an incredible display of power, Paris' father lunged in the demon's direction, daring to get farther from her. Thankfully the range of the light enabled her to see him as he spun, rotating the two blades around him, overhead and at his midsection. The demon was fast, but Stefan was faster, bursting through the air and catching the monster with both blades.

This time blood spilled to the floor in heavy amounts, but Paris only heard it, unable to see her feet. The monster screamed with real pain in its voice, but it was gone again, not moving as fast.

Low in a lunge, Stefan looked back and forth as if he'd lost sight of which direction the creature had gone when it retreated.

Paris felt Faraday's claws piercing into her shoulder. The squirrel was still rotating the refraction lens back and forth, trying to keep the range of light as far as it could stretch from the orb. Keeping it lit and hovering between them was costing Paris magic, but she had no other choice.

Her gaze was centered on her father when the demon made another attempt, but this time it moved at an almost normal pace. Its feet sounded heavy on the floor as it ran past as if it was half-dragging them.

That's why Paris saw the monster before it approached, again taking the path between Stefan and her.

She didn't think. Only acted, fueled by a deep instinct that moved her hand for her. The knife came up through the air, and Paris felt it magnetize to the beast's chest as it ran straight for her. This time, it was ready to attack rather than tease. It was out for blood now after being injured several times.

Unfortunately for the demon, Paris' desire to stamp out evil was stronger than its force, and she plunged the giant-made knife straight in its chest, halting it at once—turning it into a sudden explosion of fire.

CHAPTER FIFTY-THREE

The heat was instant and a huge contrast to the icy cold rising from the concrete floor.

Paris was so shocked that she jumped back, pulling the knife from the demon's chest as it ignited in flames that spread from its chest and outward, covering it. The sudden blaze would have stolen Paris' attention and obscured her view of her father if he hadn't darted around the demon in a flash and pulled her back with one arm, the swords still in both his hands.

Everything about Stefan reeked of protectiveness as he put his body in front of hers, the demon burning fast and instantly turning to ash. She'd never seen anything like it as she peeked from over her father's shoulder.

Only when the demon disintegrated did Paris realize that her weapon was burning her. She jerked her hand down and was shocked to see the giant-made blade glowing a fiery red. The hilt was smoking in her hands.

Automatically, Paris dropped the knife at her feet. It disappeared into the icy mist where it made a shattering noise.

Paris glanced up at her father, so close that even when she looked down, he was still in view. The light of the orb made his expression clear as he turned—shock covered his face as he looked her over.

Everything had happened so fast. Paris' heart was racing with adrenaline when she remembered that Faraday was still on her shoulder, having clung to her back when she stabbed the demon in the chest. He'd nearly fallen off and was clambering to get a hold on her again.

Since both her hands were free, Paris grabbed the shivering squirrel and pressed him protectively to her chest.

"Are you okay?" Stefan asked, still looking her over as though she might be hiding a wound.

In shock, with the smell of burnt flesh assaulting her nose, Paris nodded. She was simultaneously burning hot from the demon bursting into sudden flames and freezing from the still cold temperatures in the skyscraper's basement.

With the demon gone, the icy mist started to clear. The floor and their legs and feet slowly became visible.

"You killed that demon." Stefan turned and appraised the large pile of ash on the floor where the demon had been.

"I also lost the knife as Subner foretold." Paris noted the metal shards on the floor where the knife had shattered. The only thing that remained was the hilt, scorched from when it had burned hot and fast from contacting the demon. The stark contrast of extreme heat followed by extreme cold had caused the blade to shatter.

Stefan shook his head, dismissing her disappointment and frustration about the elf being right. "The same thing would have happened if I used the giant-made knife. When it contacted the demon, which was incredibly powerful, more so than most, it created a reaction causing instant combustion."

Realizing that she probably sustained burns if she dropped the knife so suddenly, Stefan sheathed both of his swords and reached for her hand to inspect it. The skin was raw and already swelling.

Paris sucked in a breath as the pain finally registered. She tried to hide her grimace when her father examined her.

He didn't ask if she was okay. They both knew that she had severe burns on her dominant hand. He released her, grabbed the end of his long black traveling cloak, and ripped off a piece of it.

Grabbing her wrist again, he wrapped the fabric around her hand. It hurt like hell, but Paris knew it was the right thing to do. They were still in battle, and she couldn't afford to be slowed down by the injury. When he finished, Stefan set his hand over hers. Warmth radiated around her fingers and palm, but not in the extreme way from seconds prior when the burn was nearly overwhelming—dominating her thoughts. The pain receded, and Paris jerked her head up in shock.

"You healed me," she said in awe of her father.

He shook his head. "No, I simply put a pain relief spell on your hand. You'll have to see a healer when we return. Hester DeVries is the best."

Paris nodded, grateful not to have the pain stealing her attention. She needed to focus. She needed to keep her father in sight. They needed to kill the remaining and very powerful demon on the top floor. Then they needed to take care of Happily Ever After College before fairies suffered any longer.

CHAPTER FIFTY-FOUR

"That was seriously impressive," Stefan said to Paris as the mist cleared and they surveyed the basement. With the demon gone, Faraday restored the lights after tinkering with a fuse box in the corner.

Paris knew there wasn't another demon in the space, feeling its energy or rather lack thereof.

Stefan wanted to ensure there was nothing else there of danger since it had been the demon's lair. Paris also sensed that he was resetting before they took out the next monster. For as calm as she believed him to be in battle usually, he seemed rather shaken. Paris realized the stress of being in a dangerous situation with his daughter after their recent reunion was a lot for her father. Then, to make it even more complicated, there was the extra degree of her keeping close and always having her sights on him.

She nodded, still in shock that she'd killed the demon on her own. It was such a gross and horrible thing, plunging a blade into flesh. Yet, it didn't feel as awful as she would have thought. It felt right and freeing and like something she could repeatedly do if the result rid the world of evil.

"I'm still surprised that I did it," Paris admitted, catching her breath as the cold dissipated from the basement.

"I'm not. You're strong and brave like your mother and have the reflexes and power from your demon blood." Stefan grabbed the other giant-made knife from its sheath and handed it to Paris.

She held up her hands, not taking the knife. "I can't take that. I'm going to lose it or break it as Subner said."

"Yes, and it will be the thing that keeps you alive," Stefan argued. "I think that's more important than losing some giant-made knives."

Paris knew he was right. After seeing the demon she killed, she felt better if she had a way of defending herself. If she hadn't, she'd be dead or maimed right then. That demon was out to kill, and her father might not have been able to stop it.

Taking the knife, Paris prepared herself for the idea that she would have to use one again, possibly killing another demon. Something had to happen if Subner predicted that she'd lose both weapons.

Faraday joined the pair, the refractor lens still around his neck.

"Good work to you, helping us with light." Stefan smiled down at the squirrel.

"I'm glad I could be of use," Faraday said.

"Thankfully, there should be windows where the other demon is in the Matters of the Heart office," Stefan imparted. "That means we won't have quite the same challenge. However…"

Paris sensed his hesitation.

"However," she repeated, drawing out the word and encouraging her father to continue his sentence.

He indicated the door that led to the stairwell. "As I mentioned before, we're not taking the elevator, so that means we have fifty flights to climb to the top floor."

CHAPTER FIFTY-FIVE

Having gotten used to climbing stairs when Paris visited her parents in the Fantastical Armory's basement, she made it to the top floor without needing a break. She realized that her endurance and strength were also lent to her by the demon blood.

Unlike her, Faraday couldn't fare so well, climbing that many flights of stairs. She took pity on him and carried him most of the way. When they neared the door to the fiftieth floor, Paris felt the presence of the demon as before. However, this one was even more powerful, and the idea of that was more than intimidating.

Paris felt the demon's energy and smelled its foul odor as they approached the fiftieth floor. It was strange to calculate a being's strength as if its frequency registered on a meter for her.

Sensing her tension, Stefan paused on the last landing to the door that led to the fiftieth floor. "Are you ready?"

She sucked in a breath and gripped the giant-made knife in her hand. Looking down at the squirrel in her other arm, she gave him a cautious look.

"Are you ready?"

Faraday gave a sturdy nod in reply. She knew that his curiosity to see demons and FGA headquarters had been his motivator for coming along on this mission. However, Paris also knew that he wanted to be of help as they slew the demons—and so far, he had been.

CHAPTER FIFTY-SIX

Paris didn't know what the other floors of FGA headquarters below them looked like. However, the one that was home to Matters of the Heart was how she pictured where the fairy godmothers and agents resided.

The carpet under their feet was bright red with black lining along the walls. Textured striped wallpaper covered the walls to the ceiling. The décor was mostly modern paintings that revolved around a theme of love. The design was both loud and refined—as if it was teetering on a line, trying to decide whether to be rebellious or conservative.

Thankfully Stefan was right, and there were skylights overhead since they were on the top floor—letting in natural light. Even if the demon there turned off the power, they'd still have light, which was a welcome relief.

Matters of the Heart was the office of the current Saint Valentine, and Paris assumed that like the White House for the president of the United States, the décor changed depending on the administration.

"There's that color I was looking for." Stefan ran his eyes over the long hallway lined with paintings of various colors but mostly done in reds and blacks. Doors were also stationed down the hallway on either side.

Paris looked back and forth from the corner of the hallway, where the stairwell had deposited them. The horrible odor radiating from the demon told her that it was close. The draw in her chest fueled her to fight the monster, hiding somewhere. The cold from before edged into Paris' bones, making her shiver once more. She was doubly cold, having sweated on her way up the fifty flights of stairs, which now turned to ice and made her cold at her core.

"The demon is down there, isn't it?" Paris pointed ahead, indicating the door at the far end of the hallway. It was different than the others—two wide with an arched style and elaborate crown molding around it.

Stefan's eyes narrowed as though something on the other side of it suddenly offended him. "Yes, absolutely."

"That's Saint Valentine's office, according to the schematics I studied," Faraday offered.

"That seems like the right place for the demon," Stefan agreed.

"Saint Valentine deserted his office and FGA headquarters when Agent Ruby made attempts on his life," Paris explained. "So it would have been empty for a while."

"It can't have too many places to hide," Stefan stated.

"I don't think so." Faraday crawled down Paris' arm and hopped to the floor. "There are no skylights in there, but there's an entire bank of windows behind Saint Valentine's desk.

"The whole space is only seven hundred square feet. I don't know of any places besides some large storage closets that it could hide. There are a few cabinets and wardrobes too, but no other obvious locations."

Stefan pulled his swords from his back and started forward. "Don't underestimate a demon's hiding skills. They're masters of it and often choose the most unexpected places."

CHAPTER FIFTY-SEVEN

The smell nearly made Paris gag when her father kicked open the double doors to Saint Valentine's office, making quite the entrance. The demon knew they were there so there was no point in pretenses and sneaking into the space—which was another surprise, like the fiftieth floor's décor.

The office was a giant heart. Despite the differing shape, it reminded Paris of images she'd seen of the Oval Office for the president of the United States. Similar to that space, the walls had wainscoting with the top half the same pinstriped design as in the hallway. The bottom half was black, contrasting against the red Persian rug covering the floor.

Also like the presidential office, there was a large desk in front of the bank of windows that formed the top of the heart in Saint Valentine's office. Thick red velvet curtains framed the glass where sunlight streamed in, illuminating the space.

Unlike in the hallway, as Faraday had said, there weren't skylights overhead. Instead, there was a low false ceiling. Each of the three-by-three tiles was a painting of scenes from various famous love stories. Paris recognized Romeo and Juliet, Orpheus and Eurydice, and Napoleon and Josephine.

Faraday was right. There didn't appear to be many places for a demon to hide. There were a few large cabinets in various locations throughout the strange space. Having a room shaped like a heart didn't make for very effective use of the area, but it was an interesting design. There were also a few doors that probably led to closets or a private bathroom.

Also like the Oval Office, there was an elegant sitting area with oversized couches in front of the large desk.

Paris pointed at the massive desk. "Do you think it's in there?"

Her father studied the space and frowned. "I don't think so." His gaze revolved around the room, pausing on the various places where the demon could be hiding.

Paris noticed something red and sparkly sitting on the corner surface of Saint Valentine's desk. She recognized it. Not taking her eyes off her father, Paris walked over and picked up the tiny heart-shaped object.

As she suspected, it was the red ruby that had been on Agent Ruby's magical pen that directed his power. She wasn't sure why, but she put it in her pocket, thinking that it might be of use at some point. It had been what had finally linked Agent Ruby to the murders, and he had to be behind the demons so maybe this piece of evidence would come in handy.

"Do you think it will come out now that we're here?" Faraday scurried into the room and searched too.

"Not if it's well-hidden and doesn't think we'll find it," Stefan stated.

"There are only so many places it can be," Paris remarked.

"True," Stefan agreed, the gears in his mind turning as he scanned their options. "But it's possible that the hiding place can change." His gaze rose until he was staring straight at the tiled ceiling. "And it appears it's a place that puts us at a serious disadvantage."

CHAPTER FIFTY-EIGHT

"The ceiling," Paris mouthed, looking up the same as Stefan.

"Of course," Faraday stated. "It will be dark, with roughly three feet of recessed space between the tiles and the actual ceiling."

"Which, if I were on my own, it would make this difficult enough." Stefan's frustration showed on his face.

Paris knew why he was irritated by this new scenario. Crawling around in a narrow space in the dark to hunt down a demon would be a challenge all on its own. Knowing that her father needed to fight and kill the monster with weapons would make it even more difficult. However, they had the added complexity that she had to see her father at all times.

Him going up to the ceiling would put him out of sight for a moment before she could join him. The pair on the false ceiling in the dark wasn't an ideal scenario.

"Maybe we can draw it down," Paris mused. At this, there was scurrying above them. The demon moved fast from one end of the ceiling to the other and back again. The tiles shook from its movement, although it sounded to be moving relatively lightly.

Stefan shook his head. "Something tells me it knows it's safe up there. We're the ones who want it dead but with all the disadvantages in hunting it from here."

"What if you didn't need to be up there to kill it?" Faraday offered, seeming to be working something out as his eyes danced back and forth.

"Well, I can't see it from down here," Stefan whispered tersely.

"No, and up there, it will be difficult to fight as there's limited space." Faraday held the refraction lens in one of his paws. "What if I could be your eyes and indicate where you..." He held up his other paw and repeatedly made a stabbing motion at the ceiling.

Triumph jumped to Stefan's expression as he smiled at the talking squirrel. "That's genius and might work."

CHAPTER FIFTY-NINE

Paris wasn't entirely sure how this plan would work, but she liked the idea of her father and her staying on the floor rather than climbing through the false ceiling.

Faraday climbed up the velvet curtains to the rod where the ceiling tile met the wall. He gave the pair standing in the front of the large desk a tentative look.

As a squirrel, Faraday should go unnoticed by the demon who feasted off the energy of mortals and fairies. Also, due to his size, he shouldn't be noticed when he entered its space. However, Paris thought a distraction might be helpful.

She hurried backward to the door where they'd entered on the opposite side of the office, not taking her eyes off her father. Two flag poles stood on either side of the entrance. One flag said Matters of the Heart with Saint Valentine's crest on it. The other said Fairy Godmother Agency with a heart on it.

Picking up the pole for Matters of the Heart, Paris lifted it higher. Her father gave her a confused look, but Faraday flashed her a smile and nodded, understanding that she would serve as a diversion for him.

Drawing in a breath, Paris hoisted the pole until it knocked the ceiling tile up and out of place, clattering onto one beside it and creating a black hole. The demon screamed overhead—a painfully piercing sound. It hurried across the false ceiling, again making them shudder.

As she'd expected, the demon charged to the side, on the far right side of the room. Faraday seized the opportunity to lift the panel next to the windows and climb onto the false ceiling. He only had to move it a few inches to get through. Hopefully, the amount of light that filtered up would be enough for him to see the demon's location but not enough for it to see him. Paris prayed that the demon thought the moving section near the window was a result of her actions with the pole, not the squirrel's activities.

Now the question she had was how the talking squirrel would indicate the demon's location so her father could take it down. She stood with her back pressed against the wall, keeping her eyes on her father, knowing the next part was up to him.

CHAPTER SIXTY

Stefan stealthily moved under the area where the demon paused after being spooked. It was only a guess since they all knew that it could have changed locations without making a noise or movement once it had sped to the far side of the false ceiling. That's why Faraday's role was pivotal. Stefan could stab the panels randomly, but the odds of hitting the demon would be slim. There was too much space to cover, and the monster moved so quickly. It would be like playing Whack-A-Mole without knowing where to whack.

Paris still didn't know how Faraday would communicate the demon's location when a strange beam of light that almost went unnoticed in the bright sun-filled office streamed down from the ceiling a few feet from her father.

Of course, Paris thought, realizing that one of the things the refraction lens must be able to do was bend light. The clever squirrel must have used the light by his location to direct it at the demon and down to the office, indicating where the monster was. It was strange magitech but devilishly helpful for their purposes.

The beam of light would be hard to see if one was beside it. However, from Paris' place by the wall, she had a clear view of it. Stefan was too close, though, and she knew he hadn't seen it.

"Dad," Paris whispered, pointing at where the beam of light was shooting down from the ceiling a few yards from where he stood.

He looked up and around, then to the carpet where it was easier to see the spot the light made on the dark carpet. Nodding, Stefan figured out how Faraday was communicating the sneaky demon's location above.

He grinned, striding over, straight underneath the light, holding the swords in both his hands at the ready.

CHAPTER SIXTY-ONE

In a swift movement, Stefan thrust one sword above his head, piercing through the painted ceiling tile. A howl so loud it rang in Paris' head made her think it would explode from the impact that sounded through the air.

Stefan yanked the sword down, and there was an unmistakable dash above them as the demon searched for a new location. Paris hoped it didn't spot Faraday, watching from the shadows next to the slightly ajar ceiling tile.

She tracked the progression of the demon until the sound went silent as it went still again. Looking at her father, who was watching the ceiling too, Paris spied the demon's black blood on the tip of his sword. The monster was wounded, but killing it from underneath would be nearly impossible.

This wasn't the end strategy. Instead, they would hope this weakened the beast and bring it down using other means. Demon hunting wasn't an easy game, and going on this mission had made Paris understand and respect her father more.

Stefan strode over to the spot where the last tile had moved, indicating that was where the demon had paused. However, as Paris had assumed, it was probably where the monster had slowed before slithering to a different location soundlessly.

Waiting for Faraday's signal, Paris searched the carpet, looking for the beam of light that the squirrel bent from the open tile to the demon and down to the floor below. It was amazing what the refraction lens could do and that it had been so helpful, Paris mused while waiting for an indication of the demon's location.

Stefan was holding his swords at the ready, searching the tiles, his shoulders tensed. Paris was glad she'd been searching the dark carpet because right away, she spotted the neat stream of light when it struck the floor. Although she was searching for the light, Paris was careful to always keep her father in her sights.

"There," she mouthed to her father, pointing at it. It was only a yard off where he was, but it still required him to move.

Soundlessly, Stefan stepped under the light, putting himself directly under where the demon rested above on the tiled ceiling. Holding both swords at shoulder height, Stefan drew in a breath before thrusting both hands in the air.

The blades pierced the ceiling tile and stuck straight into something. A scream full of horror and pain cut through the air. The demon must have jumped, lifting Stefan off his feet, his swords still attached to the demon's flesh.

He jerked downward and landed in a crouch as the scampering overhead continued. The blood on the sword blades and seeping through the painted tile told Paris that he'd majorly injured the demon. That also meant it had less to lose at this point, and things were about to get dangerous.

CHAPTER SIXTY-TWO

Paris tensed, watching the ceiling tiles shake as the demon moved. To her horror, it appeared to be heading for Faraday's position, where it would most certainly spot him and take him out—knowing he was what was giving away its position.

With the flagpole still next to her, in a flash, Paris grabbed it and thrust it up, hitting the ceiling tile overhead and knocking another one out of the way. Thankfully, that paused the demon and made it change direction. It hurried for the left side of the bank of windows, away from Faraday's position.

Paris and her father watched the tiles move until they went still again. Then they waited some more.

Paris held her breath, waiting and watching for the beam of light from the refraction lens, signaling the next location. Overhead, the sound of dripping was audible—blood loss from the injured demon. Paris thought that it was about to seep down, indicating the monster's current place.

However, the creature was still moving overhead based on the sound of the drips. It was moving slowly though, not showing its progression. They were going to need Faraday's help once the beast was still.

A moment later, the squirrel came through right on cue, the beam of light projecting downward to the carpet, marking where the demon was overhead. It was behind Stefan, who had been following the sounds of the drips, but that wasn't where the monster was.

Paris raised her hand, pointing at where she spotted the light. Stefan nodded minutely at her before turning to face the location. He looked up at it, some six feet away.

Unlike before, Stefan didn't stride to the spot beneath it. Instead, he sucked in a quick breath. Then, in a rush of speed, agility, and grace, the demon hunter leapt straight up and through the air—a brilliant and impressive series of movements.

Flashing blades swept around in an arc and ripped sideways into the ceiling tile.

Paris didn't realize what would happen until her father's swords sliced through the ceiling and hooked into the demon. The force of his jump and his launch angle brought the creature down through the tile and straight to the carpet below.

The red-faced demon with many horns protruding from its face landed with a loud *thud* at Stefan's feet. He didn't waste a moment before yanking his swords from the monster and bringing the right one down like an ax. It severed the demon's head from its body, ending the beast once and for all in a bloody but necessary finale.

CHAPTER SIXTY-THREE

Even though the sight was hideous, Paris didn't look away, knowing that her father would disappear from that location and be unable to travel to Happily Ever After College.

Blood flecked Stefan Ludwig's face, and his chest rose and heavily fell as he stood over the dead demon's body, its head having rolled to the side. His eyes flicked up to meet Paris'. There was an apology in them, but she wanted to tell him not to worry. That he had to do what he did. That she understood and didn't see him as a murderer or killer or monster.

However, his gaze said that he believed the opposite. Things had evolved so rapidly with them, Paris seeing her father as the demon hunter he was known as. His job wasn't a glamorous one, but it was necessary.

"You did it." Paris finally found her voice, her throat dry.

He nodded and straightened to his full height, pulling his gaze to the ceiling where the demon had fallen through. "I couldn't have done it without your help."

"And his." Paris pointed at Faraday as he scurried down to the curtain rod and looked out at the scene below. The sight of the headless demon made him grimace and look away at once.

"Yes, good work and quick thinking, Faraday," Stefan commended as the squirrel climbed down the curtains and hurried over to Paris' side.

"Thank you." He indicated the refraction lens. "I'm glad this has so many uses. It's definitely come in handy."

"Well, we have one more demon to track down and kill," Stefan began, striding in their direction, leaving the dead monster behind. "Let's hope that it offers us more advantages. I have a hunch we'll need them to take out our final adversary."

"Why is that?" Paris asked, pulling open the door to Saint Valentine's office, wanting some fresh air away from the demon's horrid smell.

"It's the last one, and that's always the worst in a cycle of three," Stefan stated.

"That's not a nonsensical assumption," Faraday offered, giving the demon hunter a skeptical expression.

"Well," Stefan began, wiping off the blades before sheathing the swords onto his back, "these demons were sharing leeching the fairies here at FGA headquarters. The one at Happily Ever After College has had all the students and faculty to feast on all to itself—guessing that there's only one there. If there's more than one, well, we might have our work cut out for us."

CHAPTER SIXTY-FOUR

It felt surreal for Paris to step through a portal to Happily Ever After College with her father beside her. To add to the experience, the Enchanted Grounds felt incredibly different than ever before. The temperature was still perfect as usual. The sun was kissing the glistening green grass as it set over the trees in the distance. However, it was like a ghost town.

Many students would have returned home. Some faculty too. Headmistress Starr and Mae Ling would be inside the mansion. However, no one was out on the grounds, too depleted by what the leeching demon was doing to them. Or demons.

It was strange to think that one demon could be more of a potential problem than multiple ones, according to what her father said. It made sense though because one would be stronger, having feasted on the energy of the fairies. Multiple demons would be more to go after at once and possibly separate Paris and Stefan. She didn't know which scenario she preferred, but she was looking forward to exterminating the vermin and returning to normal at the college.

"It's beautiful here," Stefan said after getting his bearings when he stepped through the portal beside Paris.

She nodded proudly, looking around the grounds. The mansion

stood before them. Beside it was the Bewilder Forest that her blood had regrown. On the other side of the building that looked regal and also like it was home to the nicest grandmother in all the world was the Serenity Gardens.

Behind the large manor was the pool, greenhouse, observatory, and Mirror Lake. None of it seemed right because no fairies buzzed around, smiling and laughing, studying under a tree, or strolling the grounds. It was empty, and all Paris wanted to do was make it feel like before.

"Uncle John sent me here to save me from trouble," Paris stated, so grateful that she could share this portion of her life with her father. "However, I don't think he knew that he was doing more than saving me from myself. He was helping me to find myself."

Stefan put his arm around his daughter's shoulder, hugging her to him as he laid his head on hers. "You speak like your mother, full of thoughtfulness and poetry."

Paris squeezed tighter to her father, always grateful for when people related her to her mother. She wanted nothing more than to be like Liv—well, and also mixed with a lot of how badass her father was.

Having come through the portal with them, Faraday looked out at the Enchanted Grounds with a calculated expression. "Where do you two demon magnets sense we should go?"

Before, as her father had said, Paris had been too overwhelmed to pick up on the invading demon's energy inside the campus grounds. Plus, she didn't know to be aware of it. However, now that Stefan had told her what she was looking for, Paris felt its draw.

In unison, she and her father turned to the still young Bewilder Forest and pointed in its direction.

"It's there," they said together with conviction.

CHAPTER SIXTY-FIVE

"You grew all this," Stefan marveled as they entered the darkened Bewilder Forest.

Paris blushed. "Well, not really. It was my blood."

"It was you," Faraday argued, hopping beside the pair. "You helped to get rid of the ghost trapped here, and she destroyed the forest. Without you, Paris, there would be nothing."

"Your halfling blood will make for quite a wonderful assortment of plants," Paris' father said, looking at a strange flower that was like a sun bursting with a bunch of neon colors. She didn't know what it was and guessed that Hemingway didn't either. It might be a brand-new species.

"My demon blood made it so new, and different plants grew here too," Paris stated. "There are dragonfly riders and deadly nightshade and who knows what else. I've had quite an effect on this place."

"I have no doubt," Stefan said proudly, making Paris blush again.

It was weird to be there with her father and trying to explain what she'd done to this magical place he'd never been able to visit. For as powerful as Stefan Ludwig was and all the things he knew, Paris felt as though there was something she could teach her father. That was... well, weird and also wonderful.

The darkness under the canopy intensified as the sun continued to set outside the Bewilder Forest. Paris worried that soon they'd be cast in blackness, as in the basement of FGA headquarters, which would make it difficult to see her father. Then he'd disappear, and she'd be left alone to take down the last demon plaguing the fairies.

Stefan sniffed the air. "The monster we're after is up ahead."

Now that they were deeper into the Bewilder Forest and closer to the demon, Paris could smell its horrid odor. She nodded, feeling the tug at her core, directing her to the creature.

The forest had already grown so much since the last time she'd visited. The trees towered overhead, and their fresh green canopy of leaves provided a lot of coverage. Various plants covered the ground, and so far, Hemingway hadn't cut a path leading through the forest. That meant they had to step through dense foliage and vines as they neared the monster they were hunting.

Many of the tree trunks were already quite large, and they were also close together. However, this location, as whimsical as it was, filled Paris with dread. It wasn't like the open space of the basement at FGA or Saint Valentine's office at Matters of the Heart. There were so many ways to lose her father and not have her sights on him, and then…he'd be kicked out of the location.

As though sensing her trepidation, Stefan reached down and grabbed his daughter's hand, squeezing it. "I'll stay close. I promise. I'm not going anywhere, Paris."

She squeezed his hand in return and gave him a confident look. "Yeah, I know. We're in this together until it's over."

"Until it's over," he repeated as a demon's scream ripped through the night air, and something took off, charging straight in their direction.

CHAPTER SIXTY-SIX

Stefan released Paris' hand, instinctively drawing his swords from their scabbards. She pulled the giant-made knife from the sheath her father had given her. The demon was no doubt charging in their direction. It would be seconds until the fight was on, but in the thick of the forest, Paris worried what that would entail. It would be impossible to keep sights on her father inside the dense trees of the Bewilder Forest.

Jerking her head down, Paris gave Faraday an urgent look. He read it immediately and began working with the refraction lens. "I'm going to try something. I don't know if it will work or how long, but it might help."

She nodded, bringing her attention back to her father and the sound of running footsteps approaching quickly. The demon was almost there, which meant the fight was almost upon them. Paris hoped it was a swift and easy kill and that fairies would be returning to their lives, but she knew there was a lot to overcome first.

The red-faced demon's head caught Paris' attention through the trees. The monster was racing in their direction as if it wanted this fight. It bared its white teeth and jerked its arms back and forth as it sprinted, leaping over plants and bushes.

Paris braced herself for a hand-to-hand combat fight, but Stefan shook his head beside her.

"They never face a fight fairly," he seethed, staring at the approaching beast. "This will be a trick."

"How so?" Paris wondered what the demon could be up to.

Then she heard the buzzing and flapping of hundreds of wings. She worried that the dragonfly riders had somehow been thrown into this fight unknowingly. However, then Paris spotted the swarm behind the demon. She only caught sight of a few of the creatures distinct from the rest to know that it wasn't a blanket of monsters.

It was moths. Hundreds or maybe thousands of moths. They were the wall behind the demon streaking straight in their direction. Paris had never feared moths until that moment, but right then, she didn't fear anything more. She didn't know what they could do to her, but as they soared after the demon, its backup in a way, she didn't want to find out. There was something very, very wrong about the moths trailing the monster.

Paris' father must have jumped to that assumption too, because he grabbed her hand and yanked her in the opposite direction, pulling her through the forest, away from the demon and its flying sidekicks.

CHAPTER SIXTY-SEVEN

As fast as Paris was, she had trouble keeping up with her father. He was incredibly swift and half-dragged her through the Bewilder Forest as the swarm of moths followed the angry demon.

Since they'd had no choice but to leave Faraday behind, Paris hoped that he'd moved to a safe place. The squirrel was pretty good about self-preservation, so she assumed he'd found a secure location. She also hoped that he worked out whatever he was trying to do to help them because at this point, they could use a solution.

Things had quickly shifted with Paris and her father fleeing the demon and moths instead of hunting them. They quickly neared the wide stream where Paris had met Edison, Curie, and Faraday, reuniting the first two with their human forms. She didn't think they could leap over the water, which meant they'd come to a dead-end of sorts.

However, her father tugged her harder, looking at her urgently. "Hold your breath for as long as you can. Don't come up until I tell you."

She nodded, not knowing what he meant until she put it all together.

In unison, the pair jumped off the bank and clawed through the air, trying to get distance to the middle of the stream, the deepest section. They both plunged into the cool water and sank low, still holding hands.

Paris turned her full attention to her father, watching as bubbles spilled from his mouth and his eyes looked up to the surface. Right then, the swarm of moths streaked overhead, spilling over the stream as though they were still pursuing something heading in that direction.

The demon didn't pass, and Paris assumed that it was on the banks waiting for them. Unlike the other two, this demon wanted to fight. It was stronger and smarter than the other two, which gripped Paris with fear.

Her father held her on the streambed as they looked up at the clear surface, waiting for the last of the moths to pass so they could rise for air.

CHAPTER SIXTY-EIGHT

When Paris and her father surfaced from the stream, there were three things evident. The moths had passed. The demon was waiting for them. And something was totally different.

The sound of the moths had receded into the distance of the Bewilder Forest. The demon lurked on the bank, crouched and ready to pounce. The tree trunks in the forest had a mirrored quality, casting strange reflections that bounced back and forth.

That must have been what Faraday was working on with the refraction lens, Paris thought. She saw how that would help ensure she kept her father in view.

Stefan spotted the mirrored surfaces all around them as they swam for the bank opposite where the demon was lurking, drool spilling over his fangs and down his pointy chin. Of the ones Paris had seen, this one was the ugliest, and that was saying a lot.

Apparently, the demon had some manners because it waited until the pair had clambered onto the bank before it stood to full height, which was about seven feet tall. Then it bent its knees and leapt across the stream, landing between Paris and Stefan.

They broke apart at once, Paris falling back on her butt and Stefan stumbling back as he pulled his swords to fight the monster.

However, now that the demon was facing the hunter, he didn't appear to want him. Instead, it seemed he wanted to play cat and mouse. The demon took off, streaking through the mirrored forest.

Stefan glanced at his daughter, his eyes full of fury. "Can you keep up? Follow me? I have to chase that thing, or this will go on until he's exhausted us."

Paris looked out at the mirrored forest, seeing that there were multiple ways she could see an image of her dad. That's all she needed to do, according to Tiffer's warning. With conviction, she nodded, not wanting the demon to get away when they were so close to ending it.

"Yes, go," she encouraged, pointing toward the retreating demon. "I'll be right behind you. Take that monster down."

Stefan nodded and sprinted through the forest with Paris quickly on his heels.

CHAPTER SIXTY-NINE

The mirrored surfaces of the tree trunks definitely made it easier for Paris to keep an eye on her father. Without that, it would have been impossible because he was fast. She was quick, thanks to sharing his demon blood, but would soon lose to her father in a race. Since he was sprinting after a demon, he'd kicked it into high gear to ensure the monster didn't get away.

Stefan was soon yards ahead of Paris, easily maneuvering the overgrown forest, leaping over plants and vines. She stumbled many times but kept up as best she could. The reflective surfaces of the tree trunks made it so that Paris could see her father even though he was getting ahead of her more and more.

She kept her eyes focused ahead, which was probably why she kept tripping on roots and vines, nearly stumbling many times.

Thankfully, she noticed a clearing ahead and a strange rock wall that she didn't remember from any of her expeditions in the Bewilder Forest. However, she had to remember that this place was brand-new in many ways and would have many different elements.

The rock wall had stopped the demon dead in its tracks—serving as a roadblock. The monster spun to face Stefan, snarling to intimidate him. However, the Warrior wasn't in the mood for it, and his next movements proved that.

With a spinning movement, the demon hunter released the sword in his right hand, throwing it in rotation forward. The whites of the demon's eyes were a stark contrast to its red skin as it realized that it had no time to avoid what was coming.

The blade spiraled through the air several times before lopping off the creature's head, spraying black blood over the Bewilder Forest. The demon's body stayed upright for a moment like a chicken still alive after someone chopped its head off. Then, as if finally realizing it was dead, the body fell hard to the forest floor like a domino.

CHAPTER SEVENTY

Paris' feet slowed as she took in the sight before her. Because of the many mirrored surfaces, it took her a minute to figure out which version of her father was the right one. She felt as though she was in a funhouse and surrounded by fake images.

However, the images all around Stefan dulled, returning to their normal appearance of tree trunks and things in the Bewilder Forest until only one demon hunter remained in front of her.

They had done it, Paris realized as her feet brought her closer to her father, who had his back to her and was appraising the dead demon in front of him—probably ensuring it was dead.

To Paris' relief, there wasn't another draw from a demon somewhere in the Bewilder Forest. There must have only been one.

Stefan turned as Paris approached, the giant-made knife still in her hand. She was relieved she hadn't lost it and couldn't wait to rub that in Subner's grumpy face.

Offering her father a smile, she kept her eyes off the bloody headless demon behind him. She was about to congratulate him when she realized that she was out of breath from running and sucked in a giant inhale. That's when she noticed that he seemed breathless suddenly too.

Or in shock. Or alarmed. Or both.

A look of confusion crossed his face as he looked at her...no, past her. Paris wondered if the mirrored images Faraday had created using the refraction lens were still playing tricks behind her.

Paris blinked, trying to decipher her father's expression until a chilling voice echoed behind her, only feet away.

"You might have gotten rid of the demons," a man said, his tone threatening. "But you're who I really wanted in the first place."

CHAPTER SEVENTY-ONE

As soon as Paris spun to face Agent Ruby, she knew the mistake she'd made. But it was too late. The unexpected had made her not think. Now her dad was gone. She was alone in the Bewilder Forest, facing a madman who had sicced demons on the fairy godmothers.

Still, Paris had to check, so she glanced over her shoulder briefly. Sure enough, her father had disappeared from where he'd been seconds prior. She'd made it happen too. After everything, she'd accidentally taken her eyes off him, and now she had to face someone who might be worse than a demon.

At least demons were soulless and out for their own gain. Agent Ruby, as far as Paris could tell, was seriously misguided, thinking he was serving the greater purpose and rationalizing his wretched behavior in the name of love. Paris somehow thought that was worse than being driven by evil. You knew what to expect with demons, but Agent Ruby would lie, cheat and take down his matchmaking brethren because of what he believed and wanted.

Turning to face the man in the all-black suit, Paris relied on instinct as she had when facing the demon at the FGA headquarters. She looked at the fairy in the black bowler hat, wearing a malevolent grin, as her hand snapped up and forward. The giant-made knife soared through the air, straight at Agent Ruby's chest. Paris thought for a moment that it would make contact, ending the man who had created so many problems for the fairy godmothers.

However, to her shock and disappointment, Agent Ruby reacted rather fast, jumping to the side and opening a small window portal where the giant-made knife soared through before closing. The knife was gone, Paris' only weapon. Subner was right. She'd lost both knives. Worse, she faced off against a madman who looked at her with an exceptionally evil glare.

CHAPTER SEVENTY-TWO

Paris was on her own. Her father wouldn't be returning to the college to rescue her. Faraday would be deep somewhere in the Bewilder Forest, her and Stefan having sprinted a great distance away from his location. The fairy godmothers would be recovering from the demon leeching them and not back to full strength for quite some time. Paris had sent Hemingway away, the only person who understood or knew the Bewilder Forest, and who she would have hoped for as her last option.

Agent Ruby stood a few feet away, looking as devilish as she remembered when she saw his image in the mirror on the night of the planetary alignment. He was smirking at her as if he was enjoying this whole thing. Knowing the demented and deranged man, this was like Christmas morning to him. He finally got to face off with the girl who had caused him so many headaches, ruined his reputation, and made him flee his job as an agent.

"You brought this all on yourself." Paris cut him off before he could insult her, as she knew he longed to do.

"I was trying to save love. Then you showed up and ruined everything," he spat bitterly.

"Save love?" she questioned. "By using social media and phone addictions and demons to ruin it?"

"I was accelerating what will happen under the current Saint Valentine to show everyone where we're heading," he replied smugly.

Paris shook her head, silently trying to figure out her options. All she could rely on was magic, but Agent Ruby appeared quite proficient in that regard, instantly opening a window portal for the giant-made knife to soar through. Battling him would be more of a challenge than she'd ever faced.

"You are so delusional," Paris criticized. "And you're sick, putting demons here and at FGA, attacking your race and people."

"My people wouldn't listen to me!" Agent Ruby yelled, his face flushing red.

"You're the one who won't listen and evolve," Paris countered. An idea started to blossom in her head, although she wasn't sure it would work. It was the bright shade of red that had transformed Agent Ruby's face that gave her the idea.

"The demons are gone," Paris continued, putting her hands on her hips discreetly. "You've lost. You might as well give up and turn yourself in. Maybe then your sentence won't be as bad."

"There won't be a sentence because I'm getting away with it all." Agent Ruby laughed coldly. "Who cares if the demons are gone? It will ruin the fairy godmothers regardless."

He withdrew a piece of paper from the inside pocket of his black suit jacket and unrolled it. "I found something interesting when doing my research on you. I'm sure that you're aware that there was a prophecy that included you. Well, we didn't know it was you until it came to light that you defeated the Deathly Shadow."

Paris narrowed her eyes at the man before her, trying to understand where this was going.

He read the confusion on her face, and it made him grin wickedly. "You see, the House of Fourteen made an announcement recently about their Warriors Liv Beaufont and Stefan Ludwig returning to the House of Fourteen. They were also proud to announce that their daughter,

Paris Beaufont defeated the evil Deathly Shadow, and she was the one in the prophecy who was supposed to face him. Still having my access to the Great Library as an agent, I snuck in there and retrieved the entire prophecy." He shook the paper in the air. "I have a copy of it right here."

Faking a yawn, Agent Ruby glanced over the piece of parchment. "It's pretty boring, stating that your power would have brought the Deathly Shadow back to life. That part is over and done with, but the prophecy recently received a new entry."

"Recently?" Paris' heart suddenly beat fast. "How recently?"

He blinked at her impassively, obviously enjoying this scrap of power. "Recently," Agent Ruby repeated. "I didn't want to believe it, but then I realized that despite you being a total annoyance and sabotaging my efforts, you have some power as a disgusting halfling with demon blood."

"What does the new entry say?" Paris asked in a rush, squinting to read the paper, but the Bewilder Forest was too dark around them.

"It says all I needed to know to realize that I didn't have to take down Saint Valentine, FGA, or Happily Ever After College for revenge," he answered. "All I had to do was to invite some demons here and wait until you showed up. I had already been planning on having the demons leech the fairies, a slow death, but not until I read the prophecy did I realize how perfect my plan would be. You always have to be the hero, intervening in things that are above your pay grade.

"After hearing about your demon-hunter father when the House of Fourteen made the announcement, I knew my plan was more than perfect. That I would finally get my reward—even if only with vindication. I might not become Saint Valentine, but fairy godmothers will wither away and cease to exist, and it will all be because of what I do to you."

"What does the prophecy say?" Paris repeated through gritted teeth.

Casually Agent Ruby rolled back up the paper and put it in his pocket, exchanging it for the silver ballpoint pen in its place and brandishing a cruel smile. "It's pretty hard to believe. Even I didn't want to, but like the Deathly Shadow, the fairy godmothers need you to survive and grow powerful. You might be a curse, but you're powerful, regardless."

"What does the prophecy say?"

He sighed, not liking that she wasn't the best audience for his monologue. Pointing the end of his ballpoint pen at her, he pursed his lips. "It says that the halfling is the key to the survival of the fairy godmothers and their institution. If something happens to her, they will cease to exist. So if I take you out, I'll take them out. Simple. Say goodbye, Paris Beaufont."

CHAPTER SEVENTY-THREE

Everything happened so fast that Paris hardly had a chance to react. All she had time to do was save her butt.

As Agent Ruby shot a magical assault from the end of his ballpoint pen, Paris could only think of saving herself, not combating it. She dove to the side, thinking of how Agent Ruby deflected her attack when she threw the giant-made knife at him.

The attack flew by her to the side, making the dirt and plants around her explode into the air. That would have been her if she hadn't moved. Agent Ruby might be a conservative stick-in-the-mud fairy stuck in the old ways, but he proved to be very powerful. Plus, he believed that by killing Paris, he could take down all the fairy godmothers. She didn't know about all that, but right then wasn't the time for her to think it over.

She had to fight this man, but she'd lost her only weapon. Rolling over on her side before he could ready another attack, something pinched her in the thigh, and her idea from earlier jumped to the forefront of her mind. Paris didn't know if it would work, but something told her it was worth a shot.

Sometimes the best weapon is a good defense. *Disarm your enemy with their power.* She reached into her pocket as Agent Ruby threw another attack at her.

Paris couldn't get her hand out of her pocket in time so she leapt behind the closest tree, which was thankfully wide enough to shield her from the assault. Unfortunately for the tree, it severed it in two, and it teetered back and forth before falling to the side. Paris ran in the opposite direction.

In her peripheral vision, she saw Agent Ruby trailing her with his silver ballpoint pen, looking for the right opportunity to shoot another attack. He was about to get her. He was out for blood—hers.

She pulled the object from her and leapt over a fallen log, stationing herself between two thick trees in case her plan didn't work and she needed to shield herself again. Then she'd really be out of options.

With a triumphant smile, Agent Ruby glared at her. He thought he had her cornered. That she was going to fight him. Negotiate with him. He was wrong on both accounts. Paris was tired of fighting. That would never get her anywhere when it came to this. What she had to do was take this evil down with his power.

He flicked his silver ballpoint pen at her, sending another deadly attack her way. With a steady hand, Paris held the red heart-shaped ruby in front of her face, right in front of the oncoming magic.

She didn't flinch. She didn't do anything. She simply relied on her faith in magic and her knowledge of how such things worked. Then she prayed, because why not.

A look of confusion covered Agent Ruby's face as he tried to decipher in the dark and distance what she was holding. Then it computed, and sheer panic covered his face as he screamed, his voice echoing in the empty forest.

"Nooooo!" His exclamation was one of pure fear. He knew that she'd done the one thing that would disarm him. He knew she'd beaten him at his own game.

CHAPTER SEVENTY-FOUR

The attack Agent Ruby launched at Paris hit the red heart-shaped ruby as though magnetized to it, then immediately bounced off and radiated back at its creator.

Agent Ruby didn't have a chance to react. It wouldn't have mattered if he had—origination magic was almost impossible to avoid.

Paris had recently learned when studying for her exams that parts of magical instruments bind to that magic. That was true even if the object was severed, as Agent Ruby's gem had been when it broke off his silver ballpoint pen. So when the red heart-shaped ruby intercepted his magic, it would bounce back and follow the spell's creator until it made contact.

The spell hit Agent Ruby straight on, launched him off his feet, and made him fly through the air. It knocked him back several yards into a thick tree in the distance. A grunt of pain spilled from his mouth, and his head jerked oddly to the side. It was almost too much for Paris to watch, but she knew better than to take her eyes off her enemy when in battle.

When his back connected with the tree trunk, it cracked loudly from the assault. In an instant, Agent Ruby slid down the bark and crumpled in a heap on the forest floor, his death much quicker than maybe he deserved. Definitely faster than the ones he'd murdered. However, Paris didn't want to punish. That was never her job. She didn't care if her enemies suffered. She wanted them gone from this world if they wouldn't be rehabilitated and adhere to the ways of love and justice.

Standing over the dead man's body, Paris let out a heavy breath. She hoped not to have to end any more evil, but if it meant protecting the fairy godmothers, she would. If her fate and their survival were intertwined, she'd do everything she could to keep them thriving.

Paris didn't look into the wide, cold eyes of the man she'd killed. She knew he was dead. Leaning over, Paris pulled the piece of paper from the dead man's jacket, not liking having to touch the broken and evil man in any way. However, she needed to see the prophecy for herself. She needed to understand it. In time, she hoped to. For now, she needed to ensure her friends were safe and recovering.

Paris turned toward the Enchanted Grounds and headed for the fairy godmother mansion of Happily Ever After College.

CHAPTER SEVENTY-FIVE

Headmistress Starr didn't look like her usual self, but she was sitting up behind her desk with a sturdy expression as she read the paper Paris had delivered upon returning to the college.

Mae Ling sipped a cup of tea, holding up her hand when Willow extended the paper for her to read it. She shook her head and smiled politely. "I'm aware that a seer thinks Paris is a piece of our survival."

"You are?" Willow questioned, then nodded. "Of course you are."

"What does that mean?" Paris looked between the two fairy godmothers then at the paper. So much had happened in the last few hours. None of it felt real, and yet, she knew it all was and had relayed the events to Willow and Mae Ling upon returning. "What does the prophecy mean? It can't really mean me? I can't be part of your survival."

"Prophecies are tricky pieces of information," Willow explained. "That's why seers are often not trusted. What they tell can be of great significance, or it can be a whole society's undoing.

"I think the key that we've discovered over time is to ignore them. If you put too much stock in them, people try to make them happen or undo them. Usually, something awful happens as a result. Look at the Deathly Shadow. It came after you because of the prophecy."

"And Agent Ruby too," Paris related, knowing the dead man's body was in the Bewilder Forest where she'd left it.

Mae Ling nodded and sipped her tea. With the demons gone, the fairies at the college and FGA would get their strength and happiness back. Already the color was returning to Mae Ling's face as she sipped more tea and thought about what to say next. "It's best to ignore the prophecy. Or if you can't do that, try and track down the seer who foretold it and get more information. It might be in the Great Library."

"It's odd that Agent Ruby was trying to destroy me, thinking that would be the fairy godmothers' demise," Paris mused. Exhaustion started to tunnel in her mind after the long day. She'd texted her father as she ran up to the mansion, letting him know that she was okay after they separated. He was relieved, and she said that she'd see him soon once she figured out things at Happily Ever After College.

"Is it really that odd?" Mae Ling countered. "You saved us from the demons today. We owe you a major debt of gratitude. Without you, we had no chance of surviving the long-term effects of their leeching."

"My father saved you," Paris corrected.

"I believe he had your help," Mae Ling stated as if she was there during all the battles.

"Well, still, he's the reason the demons are gone," Paris related.

"It's because of you that Saint Valentine learned the truth about Agent Ruby and fled before he was attacked by one of his own," Willow stated. "You've been instrumental in revolutionizing this college. It's not hard for me to believe that you'll be part of our survival. Maybe it's in a literal sense or a figurative one, but Agent Ruby wasn't successful, and you're alive. Hopefully, that means we'll prosper. I think we're much better off with Paris Beaufont than without her."

"I agree," Mae Ling stated with pride in her brown eyes.

"Thank you." Paris' gaze drifted out the window where the Enchanted Grounds of Happily Ever After College were dark. "So Agent Ruby..."

"I'll have someone from FLEA come out and take care of things,"

Willow stated at once, referring to the dead body and the demon that Stefan had slain. "Thank you for your bravery, both with hunting down the demons and being threatened by Agent Ruby. When you offered to help, I had no idea that you'd be required to be there while Stefan Ludwig exterminated the demons, but it sounds as though you were instrumental in helping."

Paris had explained the requirements that Tiffer had given her when she told about getting rid of the demons. Then she had the unfortunate responsibility of telling how she made a mistake when Agent Ruby surprised her and took her eyes off her father, leaving her alone with the murderer.

"It must not have been easy to face off with that man," Willow added a moment later. "I can't even imagine how incredibly scary that was when you were alone in the Bewilder Forest with him."

"Good thinking on using the ruby from his magical instrument," Mae Ling commended.

"Thank you." Paris blushed. "I'm glad it worked and that I thought to take it when I was in Saint Valentine's office. It was something my instinct told me to do."

"You're excellent at following your instinct," Mae Ling said proudly. "Never lose that."

"I'll try." Paris felt a great weight on her shoulders, but also the hope that it would lift now that the demons were gone and Agent Ruby had been stopped...unfortunately through death. "I'm glad my father was able to get rid of the demons, and fairies will be okay once more."

Willow nodded. "Yes, I'll be in touch with FGA headquarters and hopefully Saint Valentine. I don't think he'll return right away, he's still too spooked and doesn't want to take chances, but hopefully, things will return to normal soon as fairies feel better. The love meter should recover once the agents and fairy godmothers at FGA can return to cases."

"I hope so." Paris stretched to a standing position and looked forward to getting some much-needed rest. She needed to message Uncle John and Hemingway and her mother, but hopefully, that wouldn't take long. It was nice to have so many people who cared about her, but it was also a lot more than she was used to.

"Oh, and Paris," Willow said when she headed for the office door.

She paused, turning back to the headmistress with a questioning look.

"You passed all your exams with good scores," the fairy godmother stated with a smile. "I invite you to continue your education here at Happily Ever After College. I think it's only a matter of time before we can proudly call you an actual fairy godmother and not one in training."

Paris smiled, her chest swelling with pride. "Thank you. I'm more than relieved to hear that. It's all I wanted but never knew until I got here."

"Sometimes we don't know we want something until we have it and almost lose it," Mae Ling offered. "That's how we feel about you, Paris."

CHAPTER SEVENTY-SIX

Hemingway would return to Happily Ever After College now that he knew it was safe. Paris longed to see him. She also missed Uncle John. He'd been working on cleaning up his electronics repair shop and putting his life back together, according to Paris' mother.

Uncle John hadn't left the repair shop since returning to the mortal world and leaving Roya Lane. Liv's message had said he was "processing." Paris made a mental note that she needed to see her uncle as soon as possible. Putting his life back in order after fifteen years of having it on hold couldn't be easy. Still, if anyone was strong enough to make things work, it was Uncle John.

Paris knew things were complicated with Alicia and Uncle John. They still hadn't seen each other in fifteen years. Paris sensed that Uncle John was nervous too after all this time. He'd get there though, and she'd help.

There were a lot of things to unravel and hopefully ravel back together from all the various lives that had changed in the last fifteen years. The House of Fourteen was returning to normal with Stefan and Liv back there as Warriors. Alicia had returned to her magitech shop in Venice, Italy. Fane had gone back full-time to his responsibilities as the Lupei werewolf pack leader.

Everyone needed time to figure out what the new normal would look like and Paris hoped she could help with that. After all, things had all been turned upside-down because of her.

As soon as Paris returned safely to Happily Ever After College, Paris called her father. Her parents were overjoyed to know that she was safe once more and that Agent Ruby was dead. She mentioned the prophecy to them over the phone, and they had offered to look into things. The seer who had foretold it was the Warrior from the House of Fourteen—Trudy DeVries. If there was more to know, she could hopefully shine a light on the subject.

Other related prophecies were in the Great Library, so it could involve some detective work as well. Or maybe, as Mae Ling and Willow had said, it was best not to focus on the prophecy. Paris could see how it would make a person crazy, trying to figure out if, when, and how it was all going to happen.

Exhausted and knowing she needed to make a full report to Headmistress Starr and Mae Ling, Paris kept the conversation with her dad brief. But what he said when she was ready to say goodbye, promising to talk again the next day, made her heart swell with pride and love.

"I'm proud of you, Pare," Stefan Ludwig said over the phone, his voice deep. "You showed a lot of bravery tonight and a lot of skill."

"Thanks, Dad. That means a lot," she had replied. "Fighting alongside you felt natural."

"That's because we're family and we work well together," he said, a smile in his voice.

Paris smiled too. "I'd like to think so."

"I love you. Familia Est Sempiternum," he stated over the phone, but feeling so close.

"I love you," Paris replied. "Familia Est Sempiternum."

Knowing that she'd passed her exams at Happily Ever After College made Paris feel accomplished. Knowing that she and her father had helped make the college, FGA headquarters, and Matters of the Heart safe once more filled her with more satisfaction than she'd ever known. Realizing her friends were all safe and soon to return to normal life at Happily Ever After College made Paris truly happy.

"According to Wilfred, my science lab will be ready soon." Faraday scratched around in his sock drawer as Paris pulled back the covers on her bed, about to fall over onto the mattress. Exhaustion was close to getting the best of her.

"That's wonderful," she mumbled through a wide yawn. "I can't wait to see it."

"Me either." His head popped up. The squirrel had made his way back to the college after getting separated from Paris and was grateful to hear that she was safe and successful in multiple ways. Beside him on top of the dresser's surface was his refraction lens, which rested beside the medal that Saint Valentine had awarded him when he and the dragonriders blocked the signal making phones addictive and disrupting love.

"You were remarkable with that thing-ama-jig Papa Creola gave you." Paris slid between the sheets and pulled the blankets up to her chin.

"You know that it's called a refraction lens," he corrected with a cough.

"At this point, I know nothing," Paris muttered and turned off the light beside her bed with a flick of her finger, using magic.

"Well, I'm grateful that I could help."

"Help?" she questioned. "If it weren't for you, I wouldn't have been able to keep an eye on my father. He wouldn't have been able to find the demon in the ceiling. And the mirrored thing was pretty amazing."

"We make an excellent team," Faraday gushed. The squirrel sounded like he'd found his resting spot after trying to get comfortable for a moment.

"I agree." Paris' eyes closed.

"I want to help more," Faraday added, also sounding exhausted.

"I know," she murmured.

"I think my lab will help," he stated. "I want to look into the technology that created those drones around the cellphone satellite protecting it. Something wasn't right about those."

"As in they were too good, and the dragonriders couldn't overpower them?" Paris questioned.

"Exactly," Faraday stated. "Whoever Agent Ruby hired to do that cell phone business was also very clever."

"As in too clever, using their power for evil?"

"Exactly," he repeated. "We have power, and some use it for good. Others for evil. Some for nothing at all. The worst is that latter, but evil is pretty awful. However, that's why people like you and me are here, so we can put a stop to evildoers."

"People..." Paris laughed.

"Well, it gives you and your sidekick something to do, and I want to find out who was behind that strange technology," Faraday explained. "I want to do so much. Anything I can to help you and the fairy godmothers and whoever else wants my expertise."

Paris smiled, enjoying the passion in the little squirrel's voice. "You will, Fare. I'm glad you're my sidekick. I look forward to kicking butt with you more tomorrow."

"And the next day and the day after that," he said, sounding ready to drift off to sleep the same as her.

"First we'll rest, then we'll save the world and ensure there's enough love to keep it going around."

"That sounds like a deal," Faraday sang as a gentle breeze drifted in through the open window.

"Good night, friend. I look forward to more adventures with you tomorrow."

"Good night, Pare. I look forward to a lifetime of them with you."

Thank you for buying the books, reading them, reviewing them and supporting LMBPN. Thanks for supporting me as an author. And thanks for putting up with my author notes.

Here we go…

Let's go ahead and start with the murder mystery in the magical train scene which was totally one of my favorites. I got the idea because I was in Scotland, as I tend to be, and the Scotsman and I were hiking around Rosalyn Glen, the setting for the end of the DaVinci Code. Apparently it's also the site of a chapel from the 1400's but whatever. Things be old in Scotland.

We are hiking in the rain, which apparently doesn't make me melt, although in Southern California, nobody believes that. We come upon this old abandoned train station under this bridge. And then this buzzard swoops down and soars along the path ahead of us, coasting just a few feet off the ground and retreating the opposite direction. It was so cool and our mouths popped open and we were like, "Did you just see that?"

Anyway, immediately I had the idea for a magical train that shows up randomly and is cued by the presence of a bird of prey. And that's how inspiration happens. More on that in a moment.

So I decide I'm going to write a murder mystery scene on a train in the book. The Scotsman asks about how long the scene will be and I say, "Oh, like two-thousand words." He just looks at me. Apparently he knew that a murder mystery couldn't be done right for any less than ten thousand words and we was right.

One of the reasons that I wanted to write the murder mystery is that we often do those when we're together in Scotland since we can't go out. It's fun and the Scotsman does his best Savannah accent as the detective and I put on what he calls my "reporter" voice because I don't do accents...well, I don't do them well.

So I get back from Scotland, ready to craft this murder mystery scene. Mind you, I've never read Agatha Christie. But my daughter loves to watch Sabrina the Teenage Witch, which apparently did an homage to Murder on the Orient Express, one time. So Lydia tells me, "You have to have a countess in the story." I'm like, you got it. Then I go about crafting the story and later retell it to the Scotsman who every time I say something he goes, "That was in Murder on the Orient Express."

Oh well...It was another homage. And mine is different enough. Did you figure out who done?

My travels often give me fun ideas like magical trains signaled by birds of prey. I'm gearing up to take a trip to Sedona, Arizona with my family. The last time we were together, I nearly got impaled when the long horns on the safari ride charged our jeep. Remember that? And it inspired the magical safari scene in one of the other Paris books.

So who knows what adventures will come out of this and therefore stories. We're going to visit vortexes since there are apparently a lot in Sedona. I thought that's where weird stuff happened like brooms stood up on their end or something. Apparently in Sedona, there's a cosmic energy at these sights. Ohhhh you dirty hippies. If you try to sell me on your cosmic energy bullshit, we might have a problem in the desert.

We are also going on a hot air balloon ride, which I will admit, scares me to no end. But it's science, right? I can rely on that, right? But wind is also a factor and I'm not sure about relying on that.

My parents booked a horseback riding excursion through a canyon to which I said, "Hellllll NO!"

I live in a ranching community here in LA. We had a horse growing up. I think they are pretty. And I'm also certain they are aliens. I have zero interests in sitting on a horse and bumping around in the desert. For me, I'd rather ride on a hot air balloon than a horse. So I convinced my sister to go to Bearizona with me where we stay in the comfort of my car and drive through a park with wolves and bears. My parents were like, you'd rather be circled in your vehicles by predators than ride a horse? Yes! Bears are predictable. They want to eat your lunch. Horses, well they get spooked and you don't know what will happen.

Look for Paris having hot air balloon adventures and fighting bears in the next book.

So, Mike, tell our lovely readers, would you rather ride a horse or a hot air balloon? Again, I'd rather be in the basket of the balloon with a wolf than on the top of a horse. Call me crazy.

Not you, Michael! You can't call me that!

Much love and Peace,
Tiny Ninja

<< This is so good, I'm stealing the beginning for these author notes!>>

Thank you for buying the books, reading them, reviewing them, and supporting LMBPN. Thanks for supporting me as an author. And thanks for putting up with my author notes.

Here we go…

I think our intrepid adventurer left me an out I'm going to take. You see, I'm fifty-something something years old and I've been on the top of a horse. Yet, I've never been in a hot-air balloon, and (for me) here is the difference.

I get up on a horse on one side, seconds later I slide off the horse on the other and me and the horse come to an understanding.

(*Editor's note: I'm surprised the horse doesn't kick you. You get off on the same side you get on from, dude! You're from Texas! Get with the program!*)

It fakes being annoyed with life and I don't wish it to become Fido's food.

A hot air balloon, on the other hand, really doesn't know WHERE the hell it is going, when it will get there (I'm sure there are magical wind calculators that have a suggestion) and finally the roar of the flames could hurt my sensitive ears.

Just kidding. I love heavy metal so my hearing is f@#@#%ed beyond compare. My ears ring like it's noon all the time so a little flame blowing up into the air isn't going to make it worse.

What it will do is cause the wolf to attack Sarah and gnaw her leg off.

So, I'm going to suggest that I got two points for these authors notes. One point for sliding out of her horrible options and a second to explain the hole in her logic how going up with a wolf is going to get her leg eaten.

No going back to Scotland for a while after that.

Back to you, Sarah, for the next book's Author Notes!

Ad Aeternitatem,
Michael Anderle

ACKNOWLEDGMENTS
SARAH NOFFKE

I have so many people to thank who make this all possible. Firstly, thanks to Mike, who really pushes me to be a better writer, coming up with the best ideas, not just the really good ones. We work together pretty well, I'd say. I wonder what he'd say… Anyway, MA gave me the opportunity to write with LBMPN a few years ago and it's been life changing. He's very supportive and really cares. Thanks Bird Killer.

A huge thank you to the LBMPN team who work tirelessly so that I have less stress. Thanks to Steve and Kelly for making my life easier and being on top of everything. Thanks to Tracey and Lynne for fixing all my editing mistakes. A big thank you to the JIT team whose feedback at the 11th hour before publishing is invaluable. Thank you to my alpha readers Juergen and Martin. Thank you to everyone who makes getting the books to the reader possible. I really can't do this without you. And you make it so much more fun.

Thank you to my daughter, Lydia, who inspires my stories over and over again. She's my muse and we are always discussing story. She's an avid reader and listens to the Liv Beaufont series at night and reads the Sophia Beaufont books with me before bed. She also reads other authors, which I guess is okay. But my point is that she's supportive of me in so many ways. I need to stay immersed in this universe and remember all the details. There are 12 book in each series so there's a lot to remember. And Lydia loves my stories and then also supports me by listening and reading them so I can keep crafting. But also, she puts up with me when I go all psycho pants during a big crunch of a deadline. I will be the first to admit that I'm pretty intense a day or two before a book is due. And she always just smiles and says, "Mommy, you can do it."

Thank you to my family, the Scotsman and all my friends. You all are always so supportive of me and for that, I'm infinitely grateful. I really couldn't do this without the encouragement of those I love. On the really tough writing days, the Scotsman points out all the things that I don't see, like my dedication to the craft or how much readers are enjoying the books. I don't know what I did to have the most loving and thoughtful people in the world in my corner, but I'm going to do everything to keep them and hopefully keep making them proud.

And finally, thank you to you the reader. Without you I wouldn't be able to do what I love. Your support means so much to me and my family. Thank you from the bottom of my heart.

Love,
Tiny Ninja

BOOKS BY SARAH NOFFKE

Sarah Noffke writes YA and NA science fiction, fantasy, paranormal and urban fantasy. In addition to being an author, she is a mother, podcaster and professor. Noffke holds a Masters of Management and teaches college business/writing courses. Most of her students have no idea that she toils away her hours crafting fictional characters. www.sarahnoffke.com

Check out other work by Sarah author here.

Ghost Squadron:

Formation #1:
Kill the bad guys. Save the Galaxy. All in a hard day's work.
After ten years of wandering the outer rim of the galaxy, Eddie Teach is a man without a purpose. He was one of the toughest pilots in the Federation, but now he's just a regular guy, getting into bar fights and making a difference wherever he can. It's not the same as flying a ship and saving colonies, but it'll have to do.
That is, until General Lance Reynolds tracks Eddie down and offers him a job. There are bad people out there, plotting terrible

things, killing innocent people, and destroying entire colonies. **Someone has to stop them.**

Eddie, along with the genetically-enhanced combat pilot Julianna Fregin and her trusty E.I. named Pip, must recruit a diverse team of specialists, both human and alien. They'll need to master their new Q-Ship, one of the most powerful strike ships ever constructed. And finally, they'll have to stop a faceless enemy so powerful, it threatens to destroy the entire Federation.

All in a day's work, right?

Experience this exciting military sci-fi saga and the latest addition to the expanded Kurtherian Gambit Universe. If you're a fan of Mass Effect, Firefly, or Star Wars, you'll love this riveting new space opera.

NOTE: If cursing is a problem, then this might not be for you.

Check out the entire series here.

The Precious Galaxy Series:

Corruption #1

A new evil lurks in the darkness.

After an explosion, the crew of a battlecruiser mysteriously disappears.

Bailey and Lewis, complete strangers, find themselves suddenly onboard the damaged ship. Lewis hasn't worked a case in years, not since the final one broke his spirit and his bank account. The last thing Bailey remembers is preparing to take down a fugitive on Onyx Station.

Mysteries are harder to solve when there's no evidence left behind.

Bailey and Lewis don't know how they got onboard *Ricky Bobby* or why. However, they quickly learn that whatever was responsible for the explosion and disappearance of the crew is still on the ship.

Monsters are real and what this one can do changes everything.

The new team bands together to discover what happened and how to fight the monster lurking in the bottom of the battlecruiser.

Will they find the missing crew? Or will the monster end them all?

The Soul Stone Mage Series:

House of Enchanted #1:
The Kingdom of Virgo has lived in peace for thousands of years...until now.

The humans from Terran have always been real assholes to the witches of Virgo. Now a silent war is brewing, and the timing couldn't be worse. Princess Azure will soon be crowned queen of the Kingdom of Virgo.

In the Dark Forest a powerful potion-maker has been murdered.

Charmsgood was the only wizard who could stop a deadly virus plaguing Virgo. He also knew about the devastation the people from Terran had done to the forest.

Azure must protect her people. Mend the Dark Forest. Create alliances with savage beasts. No biggie, right?

But on coronation day everything changes. Princess Azure isn't who she thought she was and that's a big freaking problem.

Welcome to The Revelations of Oriceran. Check out the entire series here.

The Lucidites Series:

Awoken, #1:
Around the world humans are hallucinating after sleepless nights.

In a sterile, underground institute the forecasters keep reporting the same events.

And in the backwoods of Texas, a sixteen-year-old girl is about to be caught up in a fierce, ethereal battle.

Meet Roya Stark. She drowns every night in her dreams, spends her hours reading classic literature to avoid her family's ridicule, and is prone to premonitions—which are becoming more frequent. And now her dreams are filled with strangers offering to reveal what she has always wanted to know: Who is she? That's the question that haunts her, and she's about to find out. But will Roya live to regret learning the truth?

Stunned, #2

Revived, #3

The Reverians Series:

Defects, #1:

In the happy, clean community of Austin Valley, everything appears to be perfect. Seventeen-year-old Em Fuller, however, fears something is askew. Em is one of the new generation of Dream Travelers. For some reason, the gods have not seen fit to gift all of them with their expected special abilities. Em is a Defect—one of the unfortunate Dream Travelers not gifted with a psychic power. Desperate to do whatever it takes to earn her gift, she endures painful daily injections along with commands from her overbearing, loveless father. One of the few bright spots in her life is the return of a friend she had thought dead—but with his return comes the knowledge of a shocking, unforgivable truth. The society Em thought was protecting her has actually been betraying her, but she has no idea how to break away from its authority without hurting everyone she loves.

Rebels, #2

Warriors, #3

Vagabond Circus Series:

Suspended, #1:

When a stranger joins the cast of Vagabond Circus—a circus that is run by Dream Travelers and features real magic—mysterious events start happening. The once orderly grounds of the circus become riddled with hidden threats. And the ringmaster realizes not only are his circus and its magic at risk, but also his very life.

Vagabond Circus caters to the skeptics. Without skeptics, it would close its doors. This is because Vagabond Circus runs for two reasons and only two reasons: first and foremost to provide the lost and lonely Dream Travelers a place to be illustrious. And secondly, to show the nonbelievers that there's still magic in the world. If they believe, then they care, and if they care, then they don't destroy. They stop the small abuse that day-by-day breaks down humanity's spirit. If Vagabond Circus makes one skeptic believe in magic, then they halt the cycle, just a little bit. They allow a little more love into this world. That's Dr. Dave Raydon's mission. And that's why this ringmaster recruits. That's why he directs. That's why he puts on a show that makes people question their beliefs. He wants the world to believe in magic once again.

Paralyzed, #2
Released, #3

Ren Series:

Ren: The Man Behind the Monster, #1:
Born with the power to control minds, hypnotize others, and read thoughts, Ren Lewis, is certain of one thing: God made a mistake. No one should be born with so much power. A monster awoke in him the same year he received his gifts. At ten years old. A prepubescent boy with the ability to control others might merely abuse his powers, but Ren allowed it to corrupt him. And since he can have and do anything he wants, Ren should be happy. However, his journey teaches him that harboring so much power doesn't bring happiness, it steals it. Once this realization sets in, Ren makes up his mind to do the one thing that can bring his tortured soul some peace. He must kill the monster.

Note This book is NA and has strong language, violence and sexual references.

Ren: God's Little Monster, #2
Ren: The Monster Inside the Monster, #3
Ren: The Monster's Adventure, #3.5
Ren: The Monster's Death

Olento Research Series:

Alpha Wolf, #1:
Twelve men went missing.

Six months later they awake from drug-induced stupors to find themselves locked in a lab.

And on the night of a new moon, eleven of those men, possessed by new—and inhuman—powers, break out of their prison and race through the streets of Los Angeles until they disappear one by one into the night.

Olento Research wants its experiments back. Its CEO, Mika Lenna, will tear every city apart until he has his werewolves imprisoned once again. He didn't undertake a huge risk just to lose his would-be assassins.

However, the Lucidite Institute's main mission is to save the world from injustices. Now, it's Adelaide's job to find these mutated men and protect them and society, and fast. Already around the nation, wolflike men are being spotted. Attacks on innocent women are happening. And then, Adelaide realizes what her next step must be: She has to find the alpha wolf first. Only once she's located him can she stop whoever is behind this experiment to create wild beasts out of human beings.

Lone Wolf, #2
Rabid Wolf, #3
Bad Wolf, #4

CONNECT WITH THE AUTHORS

Connect with Sarah and sign up for her email list here:

http://www.sarahnoffke.com/connect/

Michael Anderle Social

Website: http://lmbpn.com

Email List: http://lmbpn.com/email/

Social Media:

https://www.facebook.com/LMBPNPublishing

https://twitter.com/MichaelAnderle

https://www.instagram.com/lmbpn_publishing/

https://www.bookbub.com/authors/michael-anderle

BOOKS BY MICHAEL ANDERLE

Sign up for the LMBPN email list to be notified of new releases and special deals!

https://lmbpn.com/email/

For a complete list of books by Michael Anderle, please visit:

www.lmbpn.com/ma-books/

www.ingramcontent.com/pod-product-compliance
Lightning Source LLC
Chambersburg PA
CBHW020418110726
47899CB00006B/2042